AMIDST

FURY

AND

VALOR

AMIDST FURY AND VALOR

Anne J. Hill • Moriah Chavis
Brooke J. Katz • Amanda Auler
BRR Cannon • Hannah Carter
Elizabeth D. Marie • H. L. Davis
Holly Maley • Morgan J. Manns
Mary E. Dipple • Ashley Schaller
Kayla E. Green • Megan E. Parmerter
AudraKate Gonzalez • Rienne French
Samantha Mendell • Austin D. Anderson

Twenty
Hills

To Ephraim Katz as you battle your own dragon.

Table of Contents

INTRODUCTION

When I first heard about Ephraim Katz's cancer diagnosis, I knew I wanted to do something to help. Brooke J. Katz has not only published with us in the past, but has become a dear friend and prayer warrior in my life, so crafting an anthology to bless her and her son during this trying time was a no-brainer.

Why dragons? Well, for one, Ephraim likes dragons, and we had this premade cover sitting around for months, just waiting for a home. It only made sense. We also liked the theme of dragons, as a symbol of bravery, either as the dragon or facing a dragon. Dragons are either majestic, valiant creatures, or vile beasts that take a hero to conquer.

May the stories in this book soothe fury and inspire valor.

—Anne J. Hill

Dragon Warrior
Brooke J. Katz

As the dragon boy sleeps,
A snake slithers into his lair
Wrapping its lengthy body
Around the young dragon's hip.

The snake blends in with the beautiful
Black and blue scales of the dragon boy.
Sinking its fangs deep into flesh,
Venom seeps into his bones.

Pain flares throughout his growing leg,
Creating a limp in his walk.
The pain so intense,
He falls behind his dragon friends.

Until someone notices that vile snake.
A symbiote leeching off the young one.

No one can remove the snake for him
Or the venom that slithers its way through his body.
Everyone cries with a loud voice.

But the young dragon,
As brave as can be,
Trusts in the one who made him.
He snuggles into the Creator's arms
And asks for His healing hand.

His Maker reminds the boy
He will need to fight this enemy
Through many trials but he will come out
Of this battle stronger and more beautiful
Than he can imagine.

He will need to rest in his Maker
Allowing the Creator to fill his dragon heart
With His strength and provision.

The young dragon puts on his full armor.
He is prepared
For the biggest battle he will endure.
But with his Maker and his faith
He can face even the darkest of nights.

Transforming him from a dragon boy
To a dragon warrior.

THE AINGEAL

Scottish Gaelic word meaning fire or light.

MORIAH CHAVIS

Scotland, 1757

Eilidh woke to someone whispering her name.

She opened one eye and stared at her cousin, Aiden, peeking through the crack in her window.

Even though their names sounded similar when spoken, they could not be more different. His wild blond curls created a halo around his head in the night illuminated by the full moon of Samhain.

Eilidh threw back her covers and crept over to the window, being careful to avoid the board in the floor that creaked.

"What are you doing here?" she hissed.

"I have something to show you. Come outside—"

"Ma said no. Not after what happened on the first night."

After the late Laird Dugan's dragon had been taken, Ma had forbidden Eilidh from going to any of the other festivities.

"I'm not taking you to the festival. I've got something better to show you." His lips curled into a grin, a wicked glint in his eye.

"I can't go *anywhere*," she said. "I'm surprised anyone is out of their homes at this hour. What about English scouts?" Aiden's father hadn't been taken like hers had ten years ago. Her uncle was a rider, but her father had been a foot soldier.

Thoughts of her Da still made her heart ache. Some days it was difficult to recall the sound of his voice. The Jacobite Rebellion had taken too many Scots, whether they ended up at the end of a noose, the barrel of a gun, or on a ship to the Americas.

Aiden rolled his eyes. "The scouts don't come close to the cliffs, not on Scottish land. They're scared of getting burned."

"The only reason we still have a castle to hide behind is because of the five dragon riders left, but they're out looking for the late Laird's dragon! Their wives are still inside." She looked past him to the empty fields where the five dragons usually slept.

"Come on, Eilidh . . ."

"I can't go," she said. "It's not safe without the riders." The long days of finishing the meager harvest without their men and the stress of the missing dragon weighed heavily on the whole clan. The fire at the door of the castle still burned, and it would until the dragons were home.

But that didn't mean they could be reckless.

"There's still one dragon," Aiden said. "They won't cross her."

The dragon in question belonged to Lady Dugan, the only

female dragon rider in the whole clan. The beast's shimmering tail flickered on the edge of the cliff as she watched over the people.

"You have to see this, Eilidh," Aiden said. "And with your fi—"

"*Shhh*!" she said and covered his mouth with her warm hands. "You can't speak of that!"

He removed her hand. "You're not going to burn me, are you?" he asked, but there was no anger in his tone, only awe.

The fire crackled in her fingertips.

The only other person with the fire was Lady Dugan. And her son needed a wife to help them on the path to restoring Scotland since her daughter did not have the gift. Eilidh had never been promised to another. The best thing, the Lady would say, is to marry Callum, the son Dugan. He at least knew the rules of the lairdship. He could teach her to be a lady. Their clan would not forget the Scotland of the past—a Scotland they hoped to have in the future.

Eilidh's blood ran cold at the thought of marrying the Laird's son. They used to be friends—before she got her fire.

"Come," Aiden said, bringing her from her thoughts. "You have to see this."

"Aiden—"

"I'll tell your mother about the fire."

Eilidh's eyes widened. "You wouldn't." Callum knowing was dangerous enough, but if her mother found out, she would make her tell Lady Dugan. She'd have to accept her fate as the next leader of the Clan. The responsibility turned the contents of her stomach sour. And what if they started to think—no, they wouldn't.

She bore no marks of a dragon rider. Each differed in

intricacy, but were always a thick line, almost like a scar, from the center of their palms to their elbow. She couldn't be the prophesied one, the *Aingeal*. How riders got their marks was a secret only they knew, but she felt safe in the knowledge she couldn't be the one the prophecy spoke of because at sixteen, her arms were bare.

"If you don't come with me," he said, this time more serious, "I'll have to. They think we've been forsaken, Eilidh. The only reason we still live and breathe with the old lungs of Scotland is because of the little power the dragons give us. But *you* are proof we haven't been completely forgotten. Now, stop feeling sorry for yourself and grab your cloak."

Eilidh gritted her teeth and did as he requested, hiding her scarlet locks under a scarf.

She slowly slid the window open the rest of the way and tucked her skirt between her legs before climbing over the windowsill. Once her feet were on the grass, Aiden winked and motioned for her to follow. They snuck past the houses of other clan members and trailed farther away from the safety of the cliffs and toward the forest.

"Where are you taking me?" she hissed. The nearer they got to the caves, the more her hands shook.

Her body remained as warm as a summer day, but she could hear the chatter in Aiden's words when he said, "Only a little farther."

"No." She halted behind the largest tree and hugged her cloak around herself for comfort more than warmth.

Aiden turned back and grabbed her wrist. "Come on, Eilidh." He tugged her forward.

"I am not going in those caves." She dug her heels in and

let her hand heat just enough to make him let go.

He dropped her wrist and wrung his hand out. "It's safe—"

"It's a dragon's den. A wildling den," she said through gritted teeth. Even the blasted English steered clear of the den.

"And they need *you*!"

She peered at the dark opening. "What are you talking about?"

"I found the Laird's dragon."

"Aiden—"

"But she wasn't alone. She's nesting."

Eilidh's eyes widened, and she took a step back. "Are you trying to get us killed?"

He shook his head. "She's injured, Eilidh, and you know the only thing that can fix a dragon's wound—"

"Fire." A shiver ran down Eilidh's spine. "Why not go to Lady Dugan?"

"You know why. Who else would the dragon have mated with in a wildling den other than a wildling?" He took a deep breath, wisps of white flowing from his lips as he let it back out.

"Aiden!" she hissed. "To say such a thing—"

"We haven't had dragon eggs since the rebellion! She has two!" he said. "The English kill any wildling they get close enough to. It's time we protect them instead of staying on our cliffs and letting it happen. Just because they are not tamed docs not mean they deserve to die. They can be our strength!"

"Wildlings are dangerous. Their fire is dangerous. They've killed riders who have tried to tame them. That's why we have strict rules about getting near them. If there was any hope—"

"Rules that should be ignored and hope that should be strengthened. The tamed dragons are smaller, weaker. If we do not embrace the wildlings and kill them as the English have foolishly done, then it will be the end of our riders. You have the fire. You're the Aingeal."

She flinched. "Don't call me that."

The prophesied one. The one who would tame the wildlings' flame and grow a legion of dragon riders to bring glory back to Scotland.

He put both hands on her upper arms and leaned down to her level so his whispered words couldn't catch in the wind. "You know I'm right. The fire has always passed to the Laird and Lady's family, but you are not them. You are common. You will be the one to restore our dragons to their splendor by uniting *everyone*."

Eilidh bit her lip. They had survived ten years after Culloden, but how much longer could they as more clans fell to English law? They already starved for food some seasons, and half of the Highland's men had been sent to America. They needed the dragons, and her cousin was correct: they weren't as strong as they used to be.

The Aingeal. The prophecy was more than rumor. It sparked hope.

If she was the one the prophecy spoke of . . .

She straightened her shoulders. "Fine. Lead the way."

He smiled and led her into the cave. The temperature grew with every step they took into the darkness, until the darkness was sparked with firelight coming from the dragon nest. Their fire was a deep blue, one so hot that they struggled to heal themselves. Wildlings died as often as they were healed by the flame, though their tougher hides prevented some maladies.

Eilidh's breath caught in her throat. She had never seen a

dragon egg. Dragons born for riders were fiercely protected. These eggs should be, too.

The nest was consumed by flame. It flickered and licked the side of the dragon eggs, which were covered in royal blue scales. The shining color shifted every time the light from the fire curled up the eggs' sides. The mother sat next to her nest with her tail tucked near her side, but it couldn't hide the foot-long gash that ran down to the tip. Something akin to tears shown on the dragon's face as she watched her eggs.

They shook, and Eilidh's breath caught in her throat. The dragon turned toward the sound.

Aingeal.

Eilidh jerked back as the word entered her mind in a delicate, but fierce, voice. The voice of a dragon.

"What's wrong?" Aiden asked, and the dragon growled.

Only you, the voice said.

"You . . . you need to stay back," Eilidh said. "Only me."

Aiden's Adam's apple bobbed. "I didn't bring you here to go alone."

Eilidh shook her head. "I don't need you, not for this."

She stepped around the rock separating her from the dragon and took hesitant steps toward her. She held up the bottom of her skirt to avoid the flames flickering in the small space. The dragon rested her head back on the ground and extended her tail with a low moan.

Eilidh lowered herself to the ground and sat near the wound. It looked clean, and the putrid smell of infection hadn't yet set in. Her hands hovered near the dark blue scales, and she looked at the dragon's face. The dragon blinked her slitted green eyes once and then focused back on her eggs. They shook in their nest. A low rumble emanated from the dragon's chest. Eilidh looked back toward her cousin.

"I think they're about to hatch," she whispered.

Aiden's eyes widened. "I didn't realize—" She cut him off with a flick of her wrist.

"It's okay," Eilidh said to the dragon. "I will help you."

She placed her hands on the wound and called forth her fire—a burning strong enough to melt the scales on the dragon's tail and cauterize the wound. The dragon cried out in pain. The cry was so loud that Eilidh feared her ears would bleed. A fierce, new pain overcame Eilidh as her hands continued to burn. The fire had never hurt before, but this heat —this intense flame—bled all the way to her marrow. Not burning her on the outside but within with the force of her power. Flame scorched the edge of her cloak, but it did not burn her skin. Ash and smoke covered the entire room, and she yelled for her cousin to run out before he too was consumed.

Then, as the pain grew even more intense, she couldn't separate her cries from that of the dragon. She did not stop, not until the wound was closed and her ears rang.

She slumped back onto the ground, surrounded by the charred remains of her dress and cloak, shivering from the cold that now overtook her. Aiden ran back into the cave, but she didn't have the energy to tell him to stop, to wait, for the dragon might think he came to harm her.

Aiden said her name over and over until she finally grasped onto it. He placed his cloak over her shoulders. The fabric scratched her skin.

"Is she . . ."

"She's fine," he said, the catch in his voice sending

goosebumps across her flesh.

"What, Aiden?" she asked, trying to stand but needing his support.

She leaned against him and looked at the dragon. The beast's slitted eyes turned to her, and she blew a puff of black smoke from her nostrils. It curled around Eilidh's legs and warmed her ankles.

"Eilidh . . ." Aiden's voice faded away.

She turned to look up at him, but his eyes weren't on the dragon or her. They were on the nest.

Two squirrel-sized dragons lay at the center. Their scales were the same royal blue as their mother. One was a boy with longer horns curling around his face, and the other a girl with five talons on her front feet instead of four like the males. A stripe of golden scales from the boy dragon's nose to the very tip of his tail distinguished him from his sister. When Eilidh looked at them, they turned their attention away from their mother and toward her. She shrugged out of her cousin's embrace and took a step closer to the hatchlings. A stirring in her spirit felt similar to when the mother had whispered in Eilidh's mind.

It wasn't words, but feelings and emotions—a call.

She crouched near the nest and held out her hand. At the same moment, both of the hatchlings whipped out their tongues and wrapped them around her wrist. She cried out in alarm. When the dragons removed their tongues, Eilidh stared at the markings on her wrist in shock.

It came to her now: some dragon riders were chosen by the dragon. Not every mark came first and the dragon second.

And not all riders only had one.

Eilidh had two.

"You claimed two dragons," Aiden whispered, his words awestruck.

"No," Eilidh whispered. "They claimed me."

ICEBOUND

MEGAN E. PARMERTER

N O CHILD OF FROSTDALE reached the age of ten before traveling into the glittering caves of the mountain to touch Neyza the Icebound.

Except for Braxton.

Snowflakes sizzled and melted as they touched his dimly glowing skin. He stood in the whirling snow outside the blacksmith forge, gazing up at the dark blot on the eastern sky that was the Tomb. The mountain may have had another name in the distant past, but once it became the resting place of Neyza many hundreds of years before, no one had called it anything but the Tomb.

It's our tomb as well, Braxton thought bitterly. *Buried in this winter forever.*

"Happy birthday, Brax."

He turned to see Sylvia walking up, her face half hidden by

the fur-trimmed hood of her cloak. Snowflakes frosted her eyelashes as she looked up at him, and her green eyes flashed with amusement.

"Thanks, Sylv."

She grinned. "I brought you a present." She lifted her mittened hands out from under her cloak and opened them to reveal a fat strawberry.

He leaned over the gift. "Is that from your greenhouse? That's the biggest strawberry I've ever seen."

"Go on, take it. I grew it just for you."

He started to reach for it but saw his filthy hands. He bent down to plunge them into a snowbank to wash off the soot and ash, and the heat of his hands sent up a spout of steam. He straightened to face her and stifled his Gift before taking the huge strawberry, his eyes narrowing as he focused. The glow of his skin softened, and he took the strawberry, holding it to the light. Its surface glimmered like a jewel.

"Thank you, Sylv. Really, this is impressive. Yours is the best Gift in Frostdale."

"Are you going into the Tomb today?"

He grimaced. "Of course you'd ask that."

"C'mon." She gave him a playful shove. "This has to be the year you go. You're fifteen. No one's waited that long before. You need to get it over with."

"Can't I just enjoy my present?"

"Nope. You can eat it, but then we're going."

Braxton stepped into the smithy, Sylvia following. He gestured to the glowing forge. "I have work to do."

She tossed back her hood and crossed her arms. "You're not getting out of it, Brax. We're going up there. A few of the others are already waiting. They'll see you touch Neyza, and that'll be that."

He studied the strawberry filling his hand. "And what? I'll be a real man or something? My going won't change anything." The heat grew under his skin, glowing a dull red. "I'm safe working here."

"They all think you're afraid."

He clenched his jaw, and a ripple of flame swept through his black hair. "Let them think that."

Sylvia studied the shifting light that danced under the skin of his bare arms like a smoldering bed of coals. "You're not afraid of the dragon, are you? You're afraid of your Gift."

"It's safe for me here," he said, and he touched the forge. It flared with heat, turning white. "But I wouldn't trust myself in the ice caverns. Fire and ice don't mix."

Sylvia shook her head, her brown curls bouncing. "Brax, there is no way your Gift is going to melt the Tomb. Trust me, I've been there before, and the ice is glacier thick."

He stared into the shimmering air distorted over the forge. "I'll find some way to ruin it."

Sylvia tentatively laid a mittened hand on his arm. "No, you won't. You think your Gift is only a force for destruction. But look at this smithy. You build things." She hesitated, then laid her cheek against his shoulder. "And you bring warmth. Who knows? Maybe you'll be the one to end this winter." A flush colored her cheeks as she pulled away with a grin and tapped the strawberry still held in his other hand. "Now eat your present before you burn it."

The skin of the strawberry sizzled where his fingers pressed into it. He blushed and took a bite, and the bright flavor was a spark of sunshine in the winter surrounding them. "That is . . . Did you taste it?"

"No, I grew it for you. No one else."

He took out a knife and cut the berry in half. "You have to try it."

She only resisted a moment before taking the unblemished half and stuffing it in her mouth. Her eyes closed, and she took her time, savoring it. Finally, she said, "It should be the first day of summer, you know. Can you imagine whole fields of these? Buckets and buckets of strawberries?"

"I can't."

"Neither can I. But I can dream." She linked her arm through Braxton's, not flinching away from his heat. "Come on. Let's go see the dragon that robbed us of summer and strawberries."

The Tomb's entrance loomed dark above the village of Frostdale where it huddled in the foothills. Standing on the trail that ended at the gaping entrance, a group of four stood, the wind pelting them with snow. Three of them were swathed in their frosted cloaks, but Braxton stood with no cloak, bareheaded, the wind whipping his hair as he studied their destination. The snowflakes hissed and steamed as they touched him.

A tunnel disappeared deep into the mountain. Its walls were slabs of dark stone coated in thick, smooth ice. No glimmer of light invited them in. No sound whispered to them. Nothing moved, not even to threaten or warn them.

Sylvia nodded. "All right. Get your sticks out."

Braxton watched as Sylvia and the two others—Flint, a boy with a Gift for stone, and Cassie, a girl with a Gift for water—took out long knobby sticks covered with thick green moss. Sylvia whispered to the patches of moss until they glowed, washing them all in a faint emerald light. Braxton raised an eyebrow.

"Can't take torches in," Sylvia explained. "It'd melt the ice."

"But you'll take me."

She gave him a smile. "You'll be fine. I trust you." She stepped into the Tomb, her glowing stick held aloft. Flint shook his head at Braxton before following her, and Cassie gave him a wink as she handed him the fourth stick. Braxton gripped it, his fire controlled but his palm slick with sweat. He glanced back down the mountain trail before taking a shaky breath and following them in.

The wind died. Silence and the weight of the mountain pressed down on them. Their breath clouded in the still air of the tunnel, and the green light was a compressed pocket of color in a dead and icy prison. The path ahead twisted, sinuous and serpentine, before splitting into many branches. They stopped.

"I don't remember the turns. Flint, take the lead," Sylvia said. Her voice was an echoing whisper, loud in the stillness. Flint nodded, and his fingers brushed the ice covering the stony walls.

"Stone says this way." He pointed to the tunnel that dipped downward.

Braxton wondered how it would feel to have a Gift like the others. Flint conversed with granite, Cassie chattered happily with water, and Sylvia coaxed life out of the tiniest growing things. But Braxton lived a constant battle against the fire.

Their Gifts were with them from the age of ten, each of them feeling a pull, a call to something outside themselves. Most children of Frostdale found ways to be useful with their different Gifts, but Braxton had never truly felt in control of the fire. The difference between him and the others was the fire was *inside*, not outside. His skin rippled with heat all the time, and it was all he could do to hold it in. It had taken him years to master it enough to not hurt others when they touched him.

The elders of Frostdale told stories that a Gift would one day break the wintry curse and destroy Neyza, and so the children had created a rite of passage: travel into the Tomb when your Gift appeared to see if you were the one to break the curse. No child had ever succeeded in being the one destined to crush the dragon, but still the rite of passage carried on with each fresh generation.

Braxton feared his Gift would wake the sleeping menace without being able to stop it. What could one person's fire do against a creature of eternal winter?

The moss torch shook in his hand as they walked through the tunnels. Though he kept as far from the walls as possible, he could see a sheen on the ice as it melted with his passing. His heart thudded.

Why did I come here?

But still he followed, and after long minutes of brisk walking that took them deeper and deeper into the heart of the Tomb, the tunnel broke into a massive chamber. The ceiling flew away above their heads, and air moved around them. Darkness was a living thing trying to smother their weak green torches.

Sylvia's face swam out of the darkness to lean in close to Braxton. She took his hand, her cold fingers almost steaming as they touched his. "Come on."

If Sylv thinks I can do it, I can. She's right. There's no way I can bring this place down. I'm just one person. He took a steadying breath and let her lead him until they came to the center of the chamber.

Out of the gloom, Neyza the Icebound appeared.

The dragon himself was ice. His flesh refracted the moss light they carried, shooting back slivers of blue and purple, and his slick smooth scales looked as if they were carved from clear crystal. All of Neyza's pale pink and blue organs could be seen right through his skin. The bones of his skull shone white through their icy armor. Two sapphire eyes lurked in their sockets, wide open and gleaming.

Braxton staggered back, bringing up his stick like a weapon. A soft chuckle sounded close to his ear as Sylvia pulled him forward.

"His eyes are always open, but he's sleeping."

"Are you sure?" He hated how much his voice shook, and he heard a titter of laughter from Cassie behind them.

Sylvia squeezed his hand. "Trust me."

They drew close, and the heavy head, bigger than a man, hung in the air before them.

"Touch him. That's all you have to do, and we'll head home." Sylvia stepped back.

Braxton stood alone, hands shaking, heart pounding, fire simmering, until he finally steeled himself and reached out. His fingers brushed the heavy jaw of Neyza the Icebound.

Steam rose from the scales where he touched them.

The sapphire eyes blinked once, slowly, before locking onto him.

Braxton jerked his hand away, but it was too late.

A shuddering shook the chamber, and there was a tremendous crack, as if a stone had plunged through the surface of a frozen lake. An eerie singing noise filled the Tomb as Neyza's limbs jerked and thrashed, his outer layer of ice shattering in great sheets.

"Braxton, what did you do?" Sylvia grabbed his arm and pulled him backward toward the tunnel. Cassie and Flint were already running, screaming to hurry.

"I shouldn't have come." He turned and ran, his boots pounding against the stone, his feet threatening to slip. He gripped Sylvia's hand as the dragon broke open his frozen jaws and let forth a thunderous bellow. The ground shook under their feet as they dashed back into the narrow confines of the tunnel. The green moss torches wavered and shook, illuminating their frightened faces before blinking out.

A blast of cold swept up from behind, the stink of Neyza's breath pursuing them. The walls of ice grew thick with the dragon's wintry breath, closing in tight to trap them.

Cassie shrieked as she struggled to get free. "We're going to die!"

Sylvia's grip on Braxton tightened, but he pried her fingers loose. "No, we're not."

He let the fire in his chest burn. His skin blazed, shining like the heart of a forge. The walls receded, melting and filling the air with clouds of steam. He quickly touched each of the sticks, and the moss ignited into flame.

"Go, go!"

The four of them scrambled, but their feet slipped, deep

water splashing around their legs. All the ice in the tunnel was melting from Braxton's heat.

"Cassie, move the water away," Sylvia ordered.

Cassie chattered in a strange, bubbling warble to the rivulets of melting water, and the streams moved, clearing a path of dry stone. Legs and lungs burning, they climbed higher and higher, spurred on by the sound of claws scraping at rock. The tunnel leveled off, and the entrance drew near.

Neyza closed the distance, his breath a hurricane of snow and ice seeking to claim them.

"Get ahead of me," Braxton said, shoving Sylvia toward the others. He caught one glance of her terrified face before he turned to face Neyza.

"Brax, no!"

But he knew what his Gift was for now. He couldn't turn back. There was a purpose to the burning in his body and soul.

The dragon slithered up the tunnel, and the stone was recoated in ice as he passed. As his breath fell on Braxton, Neyza pierced the young man with his sapphire gaze.

"Foolish child." The voice was grinding, the sound of a glacier carving out rock. "This land is mine. Bound by ice. Forever."

"No. This winter has to end." Braxton held up his hands, and flames flared to life on his palms. His hair stirred with the gathering heat, and his skin cracked. His fingertips blackened. Dimly, he could hear Sylvia screaming his name, but the roar of the fire in his blood was too strong.

Neyza, his scales steaming in the heat, bellowed and lashed out with massive talons. They raked Braxton's body, and a fierce cold punched into his chest, stealing his breath in a rush. He gasped, trying to suck in air, and watched as Neyza's jaws opened wide. Pale blue crystals, sharp as daggers, grew in the dragon's mouth before pouring out in a torrent. Spears of ice pelted Braxton, coating his body, smothering his face. He fought for breath, but the ice leapt down his throat, choking him. The cold penetrated his bones. He grew still, and the flames guttered.

"*Braxton!*" Sylvia's voice came from far away, and he latched onto it for strength.

Sylvia's right. I can bring warmth. I can bring life and light, and I can end this.

Neyza gave a triumphant laugh and struck again with his talons, but the claws melted into nothing before they could touch Braxton again. The ice coating the young man's body shattered, shards scattering across the tunnel floor. The dragon gave a hideous snarl and lunged, teeth bared, but he shrieked and drew back as his frozen skin melted. Braxton let his Gift grow and grow, finally giving it release, the light blinding. The Tomb shook, and Neyza's thrashing and the overwhelming heat cracked the very stones.

But Braxton couldn't stop. More and more flame poured out of him. The world was lost in thunder, and his vision went white. Then black. Then nothing.

"Brax? Wake up. Please wake up."

His body jerked, and when he opened his eyes, Sylvia's face hovered over his. Her shoulders slumped in relief. Above her, the sky stretched blue and cloudless.

Braxton tasted ash in his mouth, and he coughed. Soot and

dirt spilled from his hair and skin. His entire body ached. "What happened?"

Flint's face came into view. "You brought down the Tomb, and Neyza with it. The stones told me where you were buried. We had to dig you out."

With their help, Braxton sat up to stare at what was left of the Tomb. The entire western face of the mountain had melted away. Trapped in the stone was the cracked and blackened skeleton of Neyza.

"I did that?" He stared at his empty hands, hands that had poured out fire. For once, they were surprisingly cool. The fire was still there, but subdued. At rest.

"You did." Cassie offered him a canteen.

He took it and drank, but he couldn't be distracted long from the changed landscape. Instead of fields of white, the land surrounding them was brown. "Where's the snow?"

Sylvia's face beamed with excitement. "It's gone. And I can hear them."

"Hear who?"

In answer, she plunged her hands into the freshly uncovered soil. She closed her eyes, her lips moving rapidly, and the ground trembled.

Braxton watched in amazement as first one, then two, then countless sprouts of green crept out of the earth. Faster and faster, fresh plants burst forth, rushing to make up for the countless years of dark winter. The foothills became floral tapestries, the many blooms waving gently in the warm breeze. Sylvia laughed, and the ground directly around them filled with tiny white blossoms. The silky petals waved for a moment before breaking away to drift on the wind. In their place, strawberries grew, filling what was left of the mountainside with glittering rubies.

Breathless and grinning, Sylvia pulled Braxton to his feet. "I knew your Gift was special."

A smile crept onto his soot-covered face. "You couldn't have known this would happen."

Her green eyes sparkled in the brilliant sunshine. "I did say you bring warmth, didn't I?"

"You did." He squeezed her hand, and for the first time, he wasn't afraid of hurting her. Impulsively, he leaned in and kissed her on the cheek. Her face grew as red as the berries, but her eyes danced. He brushed back one of her wild brown curls.

"Thank you for believing in me. In my Gift." Reaching down, he picked a strawberry and placed it in her hand. "You don't have to dream anymore. I brought you the summer."

Unsinkable Heirs

Morgan J. Manns

April 14, 1912
North Atlantic Ocean

I SOLDE, LISTEN TO ME!" My brother's grip on my arm tightens. He pulls me through the frantic crowd. The air is thick with screams as we make our way toward the grand staircase. "We can't use our magic here. The lifeboats are our only chance. This ship is sinking, and we both know it's not because of a blasted *iceberg*!"

I halt, forcing him to turn toward me. The crowd surges around us, desperate to escape to the upper deck. We're only a few levels from the surface. I stand firm, my will unyielding. "Alaric, the passengers . . . They're going to die because of *us*."

His eyes, the same blue as the icy water rushing into this *unsinkable* ship, bore into my own. I think he's going to say I'm being absurd. Ridiculous, even. Instead, he pulls me into an embrace and says, "We had no choice."

The ship shudders and groans, drowning out the cries of the passengers rushing past us. I muffle a sob. We did this. We brought doom upon the people of Earth.

As the crowd races up the staircase, we step aside, forcing ourselves out of the bustling throng. Under the flickering lantern light, I search my brother's face. He's always worn his heart on his sleeve—at least in my presence. Dark circles reside under his eyes. He's tired. So am I.

He runs a hand through his unruly black curls and breathes out a long, low sigh. As if he's read my thoughts, he says, "I'm sorry my portal brought us here. It all happened so fast, I—"

His voice falters, seemingly weighted with guilt that might even eclipse my own. After all, it was his decision to bring us to Earth—a world so eerily similar to ours yet blind to the dormant power buried within its core. That untapped potential was our last, desperate hope for survival. We can access our abilities here. We may even be able to return home when we are able. He knew it. I knew it. But now, this planet would bear the cost of our choices, suffering alongside us. We led evil to its very doorstep.

"You and I can get through this," I say as a wave of painful memories resurfaces. After the assassins killed Mother and Father a fortnight ago, we had no choice but to flee our planet. "You got us here. You saved us." I refuse to let him carry this burden alone.

"But their wretched creatures followed." He growls out the words.

I swallow hard, my mind racing to guess which of their monstrosities might be hunting us. A giant squid, kraken, or some other water beast. One of the assassins used his portal-making power—the same rare talent as Alaric's—to unleash one of their corrupted creations, a twisted being shaped by their dark and twisted will, to track us down in this ocean. Whatever it is, it certainly found us.

The ship groans again and I press my hand against the wall for balance.

Alaric continues, his gaze snapping to the top of the staircase, "Maybe if we get to the lifeboats, we'll survive this attack, get away . . ." The lanterns on the wall flicker ominously. I already know the plan won't work. That beast will continue chasing us, killing whoever gets in its path.

"No." I turn my chin upward, wiping away stray tears. I realize there's only one way out of this mess. "Enough running. We need to *fight*."

Alaric pauses before running a hand wearily down his face. "We can't. Not yet. Our magic is unstable here. If we unleash our abilities, we could burn out . . ." He shakes his head. "It's too dangerous. We need more time to study this place."

I clench my fists. "There is no time."

There's power to draw from here, but it flows differently than on our planet. I can feel it pulsing, just out of my reach. It's powerful, but alien—flowing in ways we don't fully understand. Without knowing its limits, Alaric is right: accessing it would be risky. We could draw from it, only to be overwhelmed, and severed from the source entirely. If that happens, we'd lose everything—our way back to our planet, our people, our home.

A woman with her hair wrapped into a tight bun runs past us, holding a babe against her chest. Another small girl with golden blonde hair akin to my own, clutches the woman's hand as her beige skirts whip around her tiny legs. My heart wrenches as the mother and golden-haired child ascend the staircase. I cannot ignore the very souls aboard this ship. They deserve a chance to live.

I tilt my jaw toward Alaric. My voice holds more authority than what I feel. "We have to try, for the people of Earth. We brought this upon them." I straighten, taking a step back. "They need our help."

Alaric tears his gaze away from the family and begins to argue, but I close my eyes and bridge the connection between myself and Earth.

As if waiting for release, power crashes into me.

The slumbering fury awakens and fiery heat erupts through my veins. It feels different, like fast-flowing magma instead of a raging flame, but it doesn't matter. I feel *powerful*.

The source pulses with its own heartbeat, adding to my own. My chest feels like it's about to explode from the pressure. It's immense. Unmeasurable. Coming from somewhere deep within the planet.

"Isolde . . ." My brother's voice fades away.

My consciousness widens. The agonized screams of passengers beyond the corridor pierce my psyche like daggers. I squeeze my eyes shut, seeking forgiveness as I block out their cries.

The source I draw from unleashes another torrent within me. It's so fast, so forceful, I can barely comprehend anything else but the power it grants me. Steadying my breath, I guide my consciousness beyond myself. I can do this. I just need to focus.

With measured breaths, I close the connection until just a trickle of power enters my veins. I breathe a sigh of relief as it returns to a creeping, magma-like state. Something controllable. I continue to let a small, measured amount trickle through.

Then, my search begins.

My consciousness flows through walls and rooms until it too is underwater. Below, I sense where it floods through the breached hull. I move toward it. Soon, I've found where the ship has been gashed open.

Studying the gaping hole, goosebumps rise upon my flesh. The beast that tore this ship open must be a hundred feet long.

But where is it now?

A fresh wave of fear races up my spine as my essence drifts farther into the ocean waters. Inky darkness surrounds me. I'm swallowed by it—ready to turn back. Then, there's movement. My heart jolts as I capture a glimpse of a dark serpentine creature. With silver scales reflected by the lights of the ship, it circles like a shark, its long, jagged tail swirling and snapping behind it.

It waits for our demise, but I vow to leave it disappointed. I'm the heir to the Golden Throne and I refuse to die.

My avatar snaps back into my body, and I gasp, clutching onto Alaric. He steadies me and I hurriedly recount what I've seen.

"They've sent a *water dragon* after us?" Alaric bombards me with questions as I sprint toward the deck. He follows, his long strides easily keeping up with my own.

"Yes," I pant, ascending the staircase. "The largest one I've ever seen."

They reside in the oceans of our planet, but keep to the underwater trenches. Our ships know to avoid those areas at all costs. They're quick, determined creatures. Kill first, ask questions later. How the assassins captured one, I'll never know. But with their influence, I'm sure this one is set on destroying everything in its path.

Another deep groan resonates through the ship. I run faster, refusing to let fear paralyze me. If we fail at distracting the dragon, there's a good chance it will devour the lifeboats as they enter the water. I can't allow that to happen.

I think of the small girl, her mother, and baby. Their image is pressed into my mind. We need to help them.

"So, how do we fight a water dragon?" Alaric asks. He seems to have accepted that I was able to touch the Earth's source without burning out.

Fortunately, I have an idea and together, we formulate a plan.

The two of us emerge on the ship's deck, breathless. The canopy of stars blends into the glassy surface of the ocean. The disorienting illusion makes it appear we're adrift in the sky.

I'm brought back to reality as crew members frantically direct terrified passengers toward lifeboats. I spot the mother crouching near the railing, holding her children tight as they cry into her shoulder. Her eyes are focused on the stars above.

Knots form in my stomach as officers pull other families apart, the men being left behind. There's not enough space for everyone.

I notice the lifeboats. They remain suspended. A kernel of hope blooms within my chest as I realize there's still time.

"Are you ready, Alaric?" We move away from the crowd.

He presses his hands together and they flare golden. I watch as he embraces the Earth's power.

Eyes widening, his hands begin to tremble. The light between his palms flickers.

My muscles tense. The Earth's power is overwhelming him.

I move closer and place a reassuring hand on his shoulder. He takes two shuddering breaths. The light steadies and my heartbeat slows ever so slightly. He's regained control. Our eyes meet and a silent resolve passes between us. We will help each other through this.

Mother always told us I'm the sword and Alaric the shield—and together we're invincible. Tonight, I hope to honor her words.

We race to the stern, finding it deserted.

"I'll draw the dragon to the surface," I say, "then it's up to you."

He nods, stretching a hand above his head. A transparent dome ripples across the water. From it, an invisibility shield materializes, ensuring we remain concealed.

The cries of the passengers, however, cannot be blocked. Somewhere behind us is that mother and her children. I don't know why, but thinking of her gives me strength. She's facing death head-on, and she has enough faith within her to keep going. To keep fighting. All while shielding her children.

Our mother did the same for us. She fought with all her strength to rid our world of those that couldn't accept our rule. Her and father gave their lives to defend us, to help us escape. It is because of them that we are still alive.

I concentrate on the ocean, glimpsing floating ice dotting the water's surface. My lips pressed together, determined. That could be useful.

As I gather ice shards with my mind, it becomes apparent I am unpracticed at using my abilities in a new world. Instead of the artful grace I'm used to, it feels like forcing opposite ends of a magnet together—unnatural and resistant. The ice barely holds together.

My brows furrow. Perhaps it's because I'm only allowing a small fraction of the Earth's power to flow through me. Back home, I could let our planet's source fill me without fear of losing control. But here, if I take it all in, I could burn out. Even now, it's overwhelming pull threatens to consume me. I shake with the strain. I'll have to make due with what I can manage—if you can call being the floodgate to unmeasurable power "manageable."

The ice eventually resembles a javelin, its icy lines pointed toward the dragon that swims through the murky depths beneath the ship. I doubt I can actually wound it. But, we need a distraction. I can provide that, at least.

Taking careful aim, I hurl the shaky ice spear toward the dragon. The weapon flies through the water faster than lightning and I watch as it shatters against its side. For a moment, I think it actually pierced its scales, but the creature only turns its head as if merely curious.

The power becomes too much to hold. I collapse, and my consciousness slams back into my body.

The scales of a water dragon are impenetrable, but I now have its attention. My forehead aches as the cold night air shimmers around us. That took more energy than it should have.

"Did you hit it?" Alaric asks through clenched teeth. The light of his shield wavers. It won't last much longer.

"Yes, now get ready because—"

The silver-scaled beast erupts through the water's surface. With its fangs bared, it soars toward us, spiked tail whipping in its wake.

"Now!" I scream.

Maintaining his invisibility shield, Alaric extends his other hand.

My eyes widen as a colossal gateway materializes between us and the dragon, engulfing it. The portal swallows the beast whole, then winks out.

Cold water sprays over us, all that's left of the creature.

"Let's see how that oversized serpent fares on a desert planet." Alaric says as he slumps against the railing. Blood trickles from his nose.

I merely nod, refocusing my attention on the lifeboats behind us. "Good, now let's help where we can."

The ship lurches, and I pray we aren't too late.

My eyes dart across the crowd, searching for those who've made it onto the lifeboats. At least a dozen are already rowing away from the massive, sinking ship. A small breath of relief escapes me—at least some will have a chance. The dragon is gone and the ship may be doomed, but survival lingers in the air for a small few.

Crewmembers shout as more lifeboats are lowered into the water. People push and shove for their chance to board.

Yet, too many passengers remain. The lifeboats are heartbreakingly few, outnumbered by the desperate souls clamoring for salvation.

"Alaric," I murmur, leaning closer to him, "can you make another portal?"

He wipes away the blood trickling from his nose. "I can try." His voice wavers as his knees buckle, and I catch him before he collapses onto the icy deck. "I don't know how big it'll be. And I don't . . . I don't think I'll be able to reach those in the lifeboats." He coughs, and I wince at the toll this has taken on him. "But I can try to save the ones on board."

A flurry of squawking birds soar overhead against a vibrant pink sky. Alaric's eyes remain closed and his breathing comes at a slow and steady pace. I catch sight of the mother wrapped in an embrace with her husband and children—the golden-haired girl cradled in her father's arms, while the young baby sleeps peacefully against her mother's chest.

Our gazes meet, and her lips form a thin smile as if she's holding back tears. She nods in my direction.

Alaric has transported us to another planet—one with a pink atmosphere and two large faint moons that look close enough to touch. They hang in the sky like distant islands.

The beach is alive with survivors. Hundreds of people, all who managed to make it through the portal before the ship sank beneath the icy ocean waters. Many still kneel in the sand, faces buried in grief. Joyful cries ring out as more loved ones are reunited. I watch with tears welling up in my eyes.

Waves gently lap on the serene beach and I take a deep breath. This may not be our home, but maybe—just maybe—one day, we'll be strong enough to find our own way back to our planet. To reclaim our throne. But for now, we must continue this fight together.

We must endure.

THE LAST
GREEN DRAGON

HANNAH CARTER

NOBODY BELIEVED IN the last green dragon anymore.

Biting wind pierced through Nadia's threadbare yellow scarf.

She tried to pull it over her nose, to keep the shards of ice from scratching her delicate skin, but to no avail. It refused to stay up. Despite her mittens that Mama had sewed with extra love—her special brand of magic—Nadia's fingers felt numb and frostbitten.

It seemed like Mama's magic was fading, just like the rest of the country.

Ruisya had once been a glittering world, full of night circuses, dancing bears, fantastical ballets, and *magic*. But then the ice dragons had swooped in and murdered the royal family and their allies, the green dragons. Any chances of thawing, spring or summer, had died in the White Revolution.

Nadia would have cried, but her tears might have become icicles on her pale cheeks.

But there had been *rumors*. Rumors that the leader of the white dragon had been spotted in the spires of Mt. Otchropa. Rumors that Princess Anya had hidden the last green dragon—the only creature who could bring back verdant springtime and end the ice dragon's control—before her execution. Rumors that Princess Anya still lived, spared from the same fate as her family by resurrection magic.

Nadia shivered again. Regardless of the truth of the rumors, she hoped one mousy thirteen-year-old could find the dragon atop Mt. Otchropa and the egg he'd stolen. After all, that was her magical gift—the ability to infuse people with hope. It was the word "hope" that Mama had stitched onto Nadia's baby blanket and every article of clothing for thirteen years. For Mama had yearned for a baby for so long. Years and years and years, and then . . . A baby whose name meant hope came bursting into the world, black hair, coal-black eyes. One who seemed to show her whole family that life still had meaning, even in the depths of the White Revolution's darkness.

The snow piled up to Nadia's soaked legs as she reached one of the mountain plateaus. A large cave loomed in front of her, surrounded by a forest of icicles as thick as tree trunks. Others hung upside down, creating the illusion of prison bars. This was where the frost-bitten man in the town center said he'd seen the dragon, not but two days prior.

Nadia blew on her mittens and hoped for a great many things.

That the dragon would be in here. That her magic wouldn't fail her. That what she was about to do wasn't as foolish as everyone believed it was.

But most of all, that spring could come again.

She slipped in through the icy bars. "Zmey Gorynych! I call upon you as the leader of the white dragons!"

A gale pounded back against her, and she pulled her scarf around herself.

Perhaps anyone else would have given up, but Nadia's magic burned bright inside her chest, as warm as the springtime the green dragon would bring.

The winter chill filled the cavern and rattled it under her feet. Nadia gasped as it settled deep within her bones and threatened to turn them brittle. Her body trembled as snow crept in some unseen crevasse and swirled around her. The flakes twisted and twirled to form something white and intangible. Nadia squinted—she could make out one head . . . two . . . no, three—a three-headed dragon.

The cold settled its claws in deep, and Nadia shook. She met his icy blue gaze with a powerful stare. "Zmey Gorynych, I know who you are."

The dragon chuckled. The ground beneath him turned to ice. Nadia shook out her boots before the glacial magic could creep onto her—only to slide a few steps forward. She swung her arms to regain her balance, and managed to steady herself before she fell.

"Everyone knows who I am." Zmey Gorynych stalked forward, all three heads pointed at her. Nadia held her ground. "I am winter itself, the ruler of all Ruisya."

She shook her head. "No. I know who you really are—or who you once were." She reached inside her coat and grasped the necklace inside. She imagined the portrait within, of her beautiful Mama, her wonderful Papa, and baby Nik. "You were once Rasputin. Human."

Shards of ice exploded from Zmey's body. Nadia covered her face with her arms, but some particles still wriggled through her mittens and stung her cheeks with their chill.

This time, when the dragon spoke, the cavern rumbled with the timbre of his voice. "Never say that name again!"

Nadia lifted her chin—not with impudence, but with firmness. "Rasputin. The man who loved the queen. That's what they called you." Nadia's finger worked over the smooth finger of her locket. The love of her family was a warmth that not even the bitter cold could extinguish. "But they were wrong."

Zmey roared. A blizzard rocketed from his mouth, and the force of it knocked Nadia off her feet. She smacked against the cavern wall and her breath exploded from her chilled lungs. Pain rushed in to take its place, and the world seemed to spin—or perhaps the wind was so rough the snow fell at a slant.

"Ignorant townsfolk, with their rumors and gossip. They knew *nothing*!" Zmey stalked forward. In this form, he could not hurt her, and he possessed no flame like the red dragons of old. He may have been immortal, but without clothing himself in flesh, he could only use the weather against her.

He had become a force of nature—at the cost of both his human and dragon forms.

"I carried no love for the queen. I served that fiend for one reason only!" Zmey bellowed.

Frozen tears slipped down Nadia's cheeks. She fought for every spasmodic breath. She just needed enough air to finish the conversation. "Because you loved her lady-in-waiting. Alyona. The woman you loved so fiercely that you were able to take on human form to be with her."

"Never say her name! Alyona's name is not fit to pass your lips." Another burst of ice exploded from Zmey. Its frozen chill crept closer to Nadia, closer to turning her into nothing but a statue. She should have scrambled away from it, but the blow she'd taken still hurt.

The tips of her boots started to frost over.

Nadia's grip tightened on her locket. She could feel the faint heat of Mama's love as it radiated off the jewelry, enough to warm her. "Listen, *please*! I know how deeply you loved her. How deeply you loved both her *and* your son. A dragon-blood —a human born with strong magic in his veins. A boy who could command ice and fly."

Zmey's body flickered as the snow began to slow. The ice slowed its crawl. "How do you know about Dominik? We kept his existence a secret." All three of his heads bent down—two with their teeth bared, while the one in the middle eyed her.

"You *tried* to keep it a secret, until he fell in love with Princess Anya." Nadia could see her breath with every word she uttered. Outside, the roar of the never-ending winter pounded against Mt. Otchropa. "But the queen disapproved. She did not want dragon-blood to taint her bloodline. She tried to break them apart, but Princess Anya was quite the headstrong girl and would not listen to her mother." Nadia swallowed. Frost stung her throat on the way down—or maybe the pain of the story pricked her emotions as she spoke it aloud. "So the queen sent her green dragons to attack. The queen used her magic to compel her green dragons to kill your wife and son, but the attack was unsuccessful. Alyona gave her life so Dominik could escape."

A puff of frigid winter air washed over Nadia. One of Zmey's head flashed its teeth, the other one licked its lips, and the third—the middle one—snarled, "You lie! The attack killed both of them."

A burst of hope threatened to leap from Nadia's heart. She longed to share it with this formidable old dragon, all three heads. "No! Don't you see—Dominik was too clever for that. Battered but alive, he ran straight to Anya to escape the palace. They knew that the queen would try another attack on Dominik's life, so they faked his death. He hid behind her walls, in the secret tunnels, but there was no time to tell you before you declared war—the White Revolution. The royal family died, along with all of their green dragons. Everyone you held responsible for your family's deaths."

"And they will never rise from the ashes again."

"Except." The world seemed to hang in the balance. The wind died down outside, and all three heads leaned closer—close enough for Nadia to touch—their blue eyes meeting Nadia's own black ones. And the hope inside of her began to melt a little bit of the ice around her. "Except one of them didn't die."

"Impossible!" Zmey whispered. "I killed them all myself. My fellow white dragons and I made short work of them all, starting with the queen and her twisted magic."

"But you forgot the royal family's magic. Some might be more outwardly powerful, but one princess had the most powerful yet quiet magic of all." Nadia braced herself against the wall so she could pull herself upward. "Anya's love for Dominik, for Ruisya, and her family would not let her die. If she perished there, Dominik would starve in the walls. Her country would never see spring again, and her family would die out. Through her love, she lived."

"Then Anya will die!" The Ice Palace shook with Zmey's declaration. "I will hunt her down and kill her—"

Nadia reached out a hand. Her mittens passed through the middle dragon's head instead of stroking it. "Would you kill her daughter, too? Your granddaughter?"

Zmey's threats and curses broke. "My—what?"

"Anya and Dominik. They got away. And Anya knew that one day, she could reclaim the last green dragon egg. The one you took from her nearly-dead hands, but the one she dearly hoped and prayed would be safe because of her love for it. That, just once, love would overcome hatred." Nadia cupped both hands under the dragon's chin, though she could not physically hold him. "And her hope brought her me, Grandfather. A girl with hope in her veins, born on the darkest, snowiest of nights. A girl to be a bridge between the two warring sides of her heritage."

The snow began to shimmer and swirl. The form of a dragon loosened and dissolved, like the morning frost when the first rays of sun stroke its delicate form. Slowly, it rebuilt itself and assumed the form of a man as pale as the ice itself, dressed in matching clothes. The only thing that seemed to hold color was his magnificent eyes, blue as crystals.

Zmey Gorynych possessed a physical form once more, tethered to humanity by his lost family's love.

Zmey seized Nadia's cheeks with trembling hands. She undid her locket, to show her grandfather the family that had persisted with love despite such hatred.

"Oh." Zmey let out a strangled cry as he saw his son's face: older than he had last seen it, though Nadia wondered how much it had changed. "Dominik."

"Yes. My papa." Nadia met the gaze of her grandfather. "He says I have his mother's eyes."

Zmey brushed his chilled fingers across her cheekbones.

"Return the egg, Grandfather. End this winter before your bitterness costs more people their lives." Nadia sniffled. "Please. Let spring return. Let yourself return to us."

"But Alyona . . ." Zmey began.

"Grandmother would want her family to be together. She would want the flowers to come back." Nadia slowly wrapped him in a hug. His form was unfamiliar to her and gelid, but it still felt . . . natural. "Papa says she always loved flowers."

And with that soft whisper, the great Zmey Gorynych, the magnificent Rasputin, began to weep. Grandfather and granddaughter clung to each other, their tears intermingling until Rasputin pulled away slowly. From within his deep sleeves, he brought forth a jade egg, the size of Nadia's head.

He gently placed its weight into Nadia's arms. "I hope your heart is warm enough to hatch this egg and bring back spring."

Nadia smiled. "No, Grandfather." She grasped his hand and placed it against the shell. She could already feel the egg quickening, ready to hatch after so many years of being denied the love and warmth needed to bring forth new life. "I hope—I *know*—you and I can bring back spring . . . together."

The Last Green Dragon was first published in a different form in
The Willow Tree Swing *anthology, released by Nightshade Publishing.*

LITTLE RIDER

AMANDA AULER

I AM NO MOTHER.

My heart longs for nothing but revenge, for the screams of my enemies, as they cry out for death, if only to escape my wrath.

'Mercy' is not a word I employ. And yet, as I stare down at the child in my home, I am struck anew.

I am young, for my kind. Eggs and the futures housed within can wait for another millenia. But this child? This human child? It stirs something in me.

Chubby legs stick out from the bottom of a too-small tunic. Small feet slap on the dust and ash of my cave.

He must be no older than two turns. What had he been doing in the woods alone before he stumbled into my lair? It is an unusual thing to find a child so young on its own. Humans are communal creatures, unlike us who prefer lives set apart. They don't leave their young, not willingly. Not unless there's something terribly wrong with them.

My eyes gravitate back to the child, commanding my attention as he beats a rock against the skull of the last human who had the boldness to enter my home.

Crack, crack, crack.

The boy giggles.

They must have left this one on purpose; he's mad.

Or, I chide myself, *he's two*. And a human two is much the same as a hatchling, minutes after entering the world. He doesn't know. He cannot know.

I stretch my neck forward, my scales shimmering in the low light. One of them catches his eye. My head is level to the ground now. The boy toddles over, clumsy and—he falls. His chin smacks the stone and blood flows from the wound.

He begins to wail.

It is a wail that conjures in me the history that keeps my ire burning. Collectors, these humans, takers of untouchable things. My scales itch at the memories of their piercing arrows and scrabbling hands prying loose my armor.

I feel smoke billow in my throat, the noise producing in me such a malevolence all I can think is to burn him, just make it *stop*. I close my eyes, wrestling the flames back to sleep; they do not control me, they do not control—

A soft touch presses my snout.

My eyes fly open and although I can't see him, for he stands so small, I feel his tiny palm on my scales. He does not try to pick them free. He does not take what isn't his. I open my maw, only marginally, so the boy does not fear, and feel the remains of the smoke escape heavenward. The flame cools and crawls back, deep in its home in my chest.

Then the boy is climbing.

I have never been climbed before. Uncomfortable though it is, I find myself indulging him. How interesting that this tiny creature hasn't a clue how dangerous I am. There is no fear in his movements. His foot finds purchase in my nostril. I have to hold in a sneeze, worried I will fry him to a crisp if I let it out.

He scrambles to the top of my head, right between my eyes, and I lower my head further to the ground until my chin and neck lay on the stone. At least falling from this height wouldn't be fatal. I roll my eyes, releasing a steady sigh as I settle onto the floor of my cave, careful not to cast him headlong off me.

The boy babbles something incoherent, laughs, and slides down to the tip of my nose. He went backward so he's facing me still, belly pressed onto the bridge of my nose, legs and arms snuggled tight against me.

It's there he falls asleep.

It's there I find more inside of me than revenge.

It's then when they arrive.

I don't have to open my lids, I can hear them outside. They're too frightened to come in. I don't blame them. No one who comes in goes out again—I make sure of it.

Well—I feel the small weight pressing into the bridge of my nose, breathing deep and sure—*not everyone, I suppose.*

I cannot keep him, I know that. Delusion is reserved for man, and I am a higher race.

I must decide, however difficult it may be. Returning the boy to them may bolster the humans to the point of fantastical stupidity—they will come back to kill me, emboldened by the boy's survival.

But to kill the boy?

I close my eyes, just for a moment, and count his breaths.

No. That is not an option either.

Smoke begins to roll up my throat as the humans outside chatter in their primitive speech. They are truly the loudest of all races and would never believe it if you told them either. I smother the fire that prods me, urging me to release it and embody that which I am.

Destruction.

Revenge.

Death.

Perhaps it was these very men, outside my cave, who stole my scales. I don't know. Snuffing out their insignificance, my only comfort in this life, forsaken as it is.

The humans enter the mouth of my cave. They must be a brave lot. They will find me soon, with this boy. I cannot let them, not like this. But how can I release him? In a mere night he has become bound to me, and I will not lose him.

Yes, I decide, as the voices grow and the amber glow of distant torches lead their way, *I will mark him a rider*.

The ritual is simple, a few words, ash spread on the boy's forehead, blood from the boy on my scales. I shift my maw, his feather-light head lolls to the side, his chin paints my scale red.

Within a breath something deep and resounding floods me, more than the flame, more than the lust for blood. A safety net, a low keen of belonging—my boy, my rider.

Startling awake, he wails, but it stirs up only empathy.

Deep inside I say the words directly into his mind as the feet of the foolish people stumble and shriek through my home.

I know, little rider, I know it hurts. But it will be nothing to you but a scar of remembrance of this day. Come find me, when you are older and you are able. I will be waiting.

Just before the torchlight brings me into view, I am gone through the back of the cave, leaving him to weep and be comforted by an embrace that is not mine. It's a pain that lances deeper than death, new and fresh and so unlike anything I've felt before.

Though he is not my kin, nor born of my blood, I have bonded to him as if he were my own.

I am no mother?

Until we meet again, little rider.

SMOKE AND ASH

ASHLEY SCHALLER

S MOKE AND ASH BLANKETED THE WORLD, laying the dead to rest. They were gone. All of them. Every man in the battalion wiped out in a single day. Derek struggled to his knees, his breath rattling in his chest. How could the age end like this? How could the dragon win? Wasn't good supposed to overcome all evil?

"On your feet, soldier!"

Derek paused, fighting to connect the voice to the carnage around him.

"Soldier!" A hand gripped his bicep, pulling Derek to his feet.

Derek coughed and blinked away the haze, forcing himself to focus on the young man in front of him. Soot and unspeakable filth coated his skin as well as his clothes, and exhaustion had aged him far beyond his years, but recognition sparked in Derek's mind. "Your Highness?"

Prince Haden offered a grim nod. "Pick up your sword."

"But . . . Your Highness." Derek shook his head, sending sweat soaked hair into his eyes. "We're the only ones left." Never in his life had Derek questioned orders. Not out loud anyway. But now? How could the prince dare to hope when all light lay buried beneath the smog?

"While there is breath in our lungs, we will fight." The prince snatched up Derek's sword and pushed it into his filth-coated fingers. "Are you with me?"

Am I?

Could a nobody like him truly make a stand against the dragon's might?

Derek's head swam, but his hand tightened around his hilt. Die in action or wait for the dragon to finish off survivors? The beast was notorious for showing no mercy. "Aye, Your Highness." He hated the way his voice quivered.

"Good man." Prince Haden clapped him on the shoulder and turned to face the vast mountain overlooking the battlefield in the dim, pre-dawn light. "We aim for the heart of the beast's lair."

Derek's knees shook and he swallowed hard. Everything inside begged to flee, but this was his prince, and as long as he had courage, so would Derek. "Aye, Your Highness."

With a dip of his chin, Prince Haden raised his sword and raced for the base of the mountain.

Eyes up, Derek told himself as they sprinted across the battlefield. The cracked earth kicked up beneath Derek's heels with every step. He tried not to think about the things his boots caught on. If he stopped now, he'd never continue. He kept Prince Haden's back before him as a beacon. He must answer his prince's call and ignore the iron tang of blood polluting the air.

The dry earth transformed to gravel and rock and the ground tilted upward as they reached the slope of the mountain. Derek's calves burned and his head pounded as pebbles slid beneath his feet.

A tremble rocked the earth.

Derek flattened himself against the gravel, heart slamming in his chest. "He senses our coming."

Prince Haden met his gaze, caramel eyes fierce despite the sweat beading his forehead. "Fear not."

Words easier said than done.

Derek forced himself to breathe and wait out the earthquake. Rocks tumbled past their prone bodies for what felt like hours, but perhaps in reality was only minutes. When all but the dust stilled, Derek and the prince stood. Dirt caked Derek's skin and dust clogged his lungs, but he gripped his sword anew. They'd come too far to go back now. If they failed, there would be nothing to return to.

That truth spurred him to take another step forward despite the ache in his bones and sorrow in his soul. His breaths came in rapid gasps and moisture dampened his palms, yet he tightened his grip on his sword and pressed onward, jaw tight. For freedom.

A gut-wrenching cry echoed from a ledge above.

Derek and the prince exchanged a look before racing toward the noise. As they crested the path, a pack of goblins came into view. The creatures belonged to the dragon, minions to carry out his will. The ringleader drove a blade through one of Prince Haden's fallen soldiers.

"No!" Derek leapt forward. He would not let these foul creatures defile his comrades, even in death.

The goblin spun to meet him and metal crashed against metal. Derek pulled back in time to avoid a cutlass to the throat. Snarling, he renewed his attack, pressing in to shorten the goblin's range. The moss green, warty creature reeked of tar and something dark. Evil. Derek drove his sword into the brute's gut before spinning to meet the attack of one of the goblin's comrades.

Prince Haden fought three others, moving quickly to keep their weapons at bay.

Derek blinked sweat from his eyes and circled his foe with careful steps. This new goblin snarled, flashing yellowed teeth. With a gurgle, the foul beast lunged. Derek deflected the blow, once, twice, a third time. Dust kicked up with their footwork. Perspiration dampened Derek's skin. A stone rolled beneath his boot, throwing him off balance. The goblin's blade sliced into Derek's side. With a cry, Derek brought his own weapon up, piercing the goblin through the middle. The action sent fire through Derek's torso, but the goblin tumbled to the ground, twitching.

With gasping breaths, Derek backed away, clutching his free hand to his bleeding wound. He'd live. *For now.*

Prince Haden finished off his opponents in a series of fell swoops, bringing the stray goblin pack to an end. "Are you well?" The prince's gaze swept Derek.

"Aye, Your Highness," Derek gritted out the words.

"Onward, then." The prince inhaled deeply, thrust his shoulders back, and turned to continue up the path, sword at the ready.

He was beginning to despise the prince's vigor. Derek panted hard, but followed.

The pair continued up the mountain, taking more care with their steps now that the dragon had deployed his goblin underlings to finish off survivors. Twice they sought shelter behind large boulders to allow goblin gangs to pass. Derek pressed against the stones, praying each time his shaking limbs wouldn't give them away. When the coast cleared, they continued their climb until the gaping archway to the dragon's lair came into view.

Derek stumbled as he took in the darkness awaiting them. His stomach dropped. Swallowing hard, Derek took a step back.

"Bravery, soldier," Prince Haden murmured.

Fire bit into Derek's stomach and he forced himself to stifle a retort. Bravery, courage, and all its synonyms be burned. Yet even as he thought the words, duty pushed him forward. He may not live if he followed his prince, but he wouldn't be able to live with himself if he did not.

The darkness swallowed them as they stepped over the threshold. Tension tightened between Derek's shoulders as hair prickled along his neck. The ominous smell of smoke and soot grew with every step, yet they pressed on. A distant beacon of glowing orange light burned in the distance. Where there was fire, there must be a dragon. Derek fell in alongside the prince. Their feet scraped the edge of the dark tunnel, rocks and debris announcing their arrival.

Heat engulfed them the closer they drew to the light.

Derek readjusted his grip on his hilt and swallowed the metallic taste clinging to his dry mouth.

Prince Haden stepped into the light and Derek followed.

The largest bonfire Derek had ever seen filled the cavern, mounds of gold forming a boundary around the heat.

"So, this is the last stand? A prince without a throne and a nobody soldier?" The guttural voice echoed around them, raking Derek's eardrums and making goosebumps rise on his arms.

A long shape emerged from the firepit, shaking coins from his golden scales. The monster was easily as long as two trees pushed together. Derek's knees weakened but he forced his spine straight. The creature's shimmering eyes fixed on him.

"Do not listen to the beast," Prince Haden ordered. "Whatever he says, stand your ground."

A chuckle sounded from the dragon's throat, shaking the cave floor beneath Derek's boots. "Come, puny prince. Do. Your. Worst."

Derek locked his feet to keep them from turning and running the other way.

With a mighty war cry, Prince Haden charged the dragon. Derek followed half a second later, shouting his own call in hopes it would fuel him with courage.

The dragon responded with a burst of fire and the duo leapt apart, letting the flames pass between them. Heat scorched past Derek, burns bubbling on his bicep. He threw himself to the ground, stifling the flames licking at his torso. His wounded side pinched at the sudden movement and he groaned.

Prince Haden rushed forward, sword slashing toward the dragon's neck. For such a large beast, he was nimble, wrenching away and then swiping out with his massive claws. With a vicious strike, the dragon knocked the prince into the cavern wall with a stomach rolling thud.

The prince did not rise.

Bile tickled the back of Derek's throat as he held his sword with trembling fingers. He moved to position himself between the dragon and the downed prince.

The dragon's amber eyes locked on him. "You are a nobody boy, the son of a nobody baker, from a nowhere town. What power do you have against me?"

Once more the dragon's voice seemed to infiltrate Derek's skull. He gritted his teeth against the sensation and held his ground. "You know nothing."

"Silly boy, I know everything. I can see it in your memory." The dragon inhaled deeply. "I can smell it in your blood. You cannot hide from me."

Derek ran his tongue over his cracked lips. "I will end you."

The dragon guffawed, shaking the earth. "Very well. Try and fight me. You will not win."

"So, you think." Derek gulped a lungful of air and ran.

With a growl, the dragon lunged forward.

Derek dodged a snap of the beast's mighty jaws only to be caught by a swinging paw. Claws raked across his chest, cutting through his leather breastplate. He slammed against the cavern wall. Derek gasped, struggling for breath.

"Give up, boy."

Never.

Derek fisted his sword and struggled to his feet. Every bit of his body ached. Blood warmed his chest, but he could not stop fighting now. Derek attacked, his sword met by razor sharp claws. Sparks danced into the air.

The dragon reared, striking out with his teeth.

Derek threw himself to the side.

An inferno followed his movement, and Derek ducked

behind a mound of coins. Flames whipped past, crackling in the air for a moment before dissolving against the cave wall.

"That's right. Hide. Allow the fear to take over. You are nothing. You cannot defeat me."

Derek held back a cry as the words reverberated through his body. He knelt, shaking, waiting for the dragon to make a move. As he crouched, Derek became aware of a distant noise. Birds chirping. Dawn approached. And where light dawned, there was hope.

A snarl forewarned the dragon's attack.

Derek braced himself for the swing of the dragon's paw. Seconds passed agonizingly slow as his heart hammered in his chest. Air swept past his cheek. Now. Derek sprang into action, cutting out with his blade. A howl rent the air as Derek's sword chipped scales and blood rained down onto the treasure around him. The dragon writhed and knocked aside the mound of coins, exposing Derek once more.

Derek's lungs seized.

Amber eyes met his, narrowing into vengeful slits, nostrils flaring in a way that forewarned fire.

One last stand.

For his family. His prince. His kingdom.

Derek raced forward and dodged the beast's thrashing tail. He leapt, sword arced overhead. Derek brought his sword down in a mighty swing on the dragon's neck.

The dragon's scream rent the air as Derek's blade sliced deep into the creature's flesh. The dragon released a torrent of fire, but his aim was haphazard. It sent the spray skittering across the floor. Derek swung again and again, cutting through the dragon's thick flesh until he'd severed the monster's head from his body.

For an awful moment, the dragon twitched, then lay still.

Victory.

The dragon who had plagued their world lay vanquished. And without the power of the dragon fueling them, the goblins too would soon return to the underground from whence they came.

Strength abandoned Derek, and he fell to his knees. It was finished. He should rejoice, but at the moment, all he wanted was his warm hearth and his parents' laughter, with his siblings gathered around their mother's table. Home. He wanted home.

A dry cough startled Derek from his fatigue. He whipped around. Prince Haden struggled to rise from the corner where the beast had hurled him.

"It's over," Derek's voice came out hoarse.

Prince Haden stood with a grim smile, one arm cradled close to his chest. "Well done, Derek."

He startled. All this time, he hadn't realized the prince knew his name. "Now, what?" he asked.

Now the prince grinned fully. "We go home. Rebuild. Heal the land the dragon has brought to ruin."

Home.

"Aye, Your Highness."

Together, the pair hobbled from the dragon's lair. Outside the dark, brooding cave, sunshine greeted the world, pushing away the darkness that had seemed to swallow them not so long ago.

Gorloc's
Gauntlet

AudraKate Gonzalez

S MOKE FILLED WITH A WISH billows up in my face, burning my eyes as I quickly blow out the candle on my dragon-shaped cake. The off key singing comes to an end.

"Happy Birthday, Jonas!" The faces of those around me are lit up with smiles, hoping to be the one to make my wish come true with whatever extravagantly wrapped gift they've brought. Even the employees of Questland Arcade, the restaurant where we're having my party, are clapping their hands in excitement as if they've known me my entire life.

Looking around the room I realize there is nothing anyone here can do to make my wishes come true. I desperately wanted to have my birthday party at Laser Lounge down the street, where you get to play laser tag and fight zombies. That place would have been wicked. But Laser Lounge was expensive, especially for a family of eight.

A screaming child runs by our table while a frantic woman chases after him. This place is like a zoo of wild children. They make it hard to enjoy playing any of the arcade games. I tried to play some of my favorites from when I was younger, but I could barely beat my old highscores because of the noise and small kids bumping into me.

Questland is family friendly and affordable. They recently dropped their prices even lower after a kid went missing from here a couple of months ago. The place was shut down while the police did their investigation. They only recently reopened to the public.

While I liked Questland when I was younger—it was where I got my start as a gamer—there's something about it now that gives it a sinister vibe. It may be covered in rainbow carpeting with animatronic dragons, unicorns, and knights everywhere, but that doesn't distract from the shadows that seem to lurk in every corner. Their slogan even gives me the creeps. "Questland: Where every quest is filled with magical fun."

Bet it wasn't magical fun for the missing kid . . .

I tamp down the uncomfortable feeling and dig into my slice of white cake with buttercream frosting. My piece has a portion of the red "4" from the "Happy 14th Birthday" adorning the top of the cake.

Everyone keeps asking me if I "feel 14 yet" and I think it's a stupid question. It literally just happened today. How am I supposed to feel any different from yesterday?

"I'm ready for presents now," I say to no one in particular. Everyone is either busy chomping away on cake or in the middle of a conversation.

My mom pauses talking to my aunt and looks at me. "In just a few minutes, Jonas." She pats my raven colored hair like she used to when I was little, brushing a curl from my eye. "Let everyone else finish up their cake and then we will get to your gifts."

My gaze catches an older man standing in the corner. He watches me with crinkled green eyes, mischief dancing in them. He's barely taller than my six-year-old cousin, probably only reaching four-feet in height.

He must work here because he's not dressed in normal clothes. A gray bushy beard covers most of his face, and a brown hat with a jingling bell at the top sits on his head. Stringy gray hair sticks out from every angle. In the center of his face, a red bulbous nose stands out, reminding me of Rudolph. His clothes look ancient, like something a Jedi would wear, brown robes that almost touch the floor. They look so worn that if you'd touch them, dust would rise in the air. He hobbles closer to where I'm sitting. "Happy birthday, Jonas," he says with a musical lilt, an Irish sounding accent beneath the surface.

"How do you know my name?"

He doesn't answer, simply smiles, showing his yellowed teeth. He must have seen my name somewhere on a party list. Must be playing into the "magic of Questland" by pretending to *magically* know my name.

After a minute of him creepily staring at me with that corn cob grin, I finally say, "Thanks," so that he'll hobble away.

"A nice stack of presents you have as well. Very kind of all these people to think of you." He's now leaning against the gift table.

How'd he get over there? One second he was in front of me

and the next . . .

He smirks. "I have a present for you. A gift from . . . Questland, if you will." He's in my face, on top of the table. I jump back in my seat at his sudden appearance. This has to be some party trick.

Is nobody else seeing this? I glance around the room to see if anyone in the restaurant is paying attention to the strange little man atop the table. They're all focused on their conversations, eating cake, or playing arcade games.

He draws my attention back to him when he reaches his grubby hand into his robes and pulls out a key and waves it in front of my face.

A laugh bubbles out from me. "Is this your gift? A key? What am I supposed to do with a key?"

"It's a very special key for a very special birthday boy." The man flicks my nose with his finger. "Come, follow me." For an older looking guy, he spryly leaps from the table and lands with both feet on the ground.

I don't know if I should follow this strange man. After all, my parents always taught me to be wary of strangers. And thoughts of the missing kid start to creep in . . .

But I spot him waving to one of the other employees, so I'm confident now that he does work here, and this is probably something Questland does for all their birthday parties.

I decide this could at least help me pass the time until I can open my gifts.

I get up from the table and follow the little man around the corner. No one notices me walking away. So much for being the special birthday boy.

We turn a corner that leads to a dark hallway, away from the sights and sounds of the rest of the arcade. The hallway feels like it goes on and on, lengthening with every step we take. The man continues straight ahead, but I turn behind me to see that the restaurant has grown so far away. I can't hear the sounds of arcade games or screaming children anymore.

"Where are we going?" I turn around to ask, but the little man is gone, and I'm stuck at the end of a dark hallway with nothing around me. I decide to go back to my party, but when I spin in that direction, I discover I'm completely boxed in. Surrounded by four walls that weren't there before.

I knock on the wall. "Hello?" A hint of fear rests on my tongue. When I hear my voice trapped inside with me, no place to escape, panic sets in. I can feel my heart restrict, forcing it into erratic beats. Sweat beads across my forehead. The dampness makes me shiver.

I press my hands against the walls, pushing as hard as I can. "Help!"

Questland and the little man have vanished, most likely leaving me here to die.

I slam my hands against the walls of the tiny box. The air has become thick and musty, and I gasp. If I don't get out soon, I'm going to pass out.

When my hands swing forward to slam against the wall again, it gives way, transforming into a black curtain. I'm sent sprawling and spit out into a dark room.

The room is empty except for an arcade game lit up against the back wall. Upbeat music comes from the game, resounding throughout the room. A mix of orchestral sounds with strings and flutes and rhythmic drums that keep the tempo. The perfect music for . . .

"A fantasy game?" I approach the game. A dragon roars

across the little screen, breathing fire at a small heroic figure holding a sword. And is that . . . the little man? Up in the corner of the game, a small icon is dressed just like the man from earlier.

I jump back as *Gorloc's Gauntlet* flashes in bold letters. The "T" in the middle of "Gauntlet" is shaped like a key. "Press Enter to Start Game" pops up. I check the control panel to see what buttons are there. There's no toggle, no "A" or "B" buttons, just an "Enter" button. There's also no slot for any coins or tickets.

I press the "Enter" button and a loud buzzing echoes around the room, growing louder and louder as the arcade game itself becomes larger and larger. I throw my hands up over my ears and a bright light absorbs everything around me.

The air whooshes from my lungs when I land on the ground, bright blue surrounding me from above. The words *Gorloc's Gauntlet* flicker in the sky. Next to me, three little hearts pop up, and an electronic sound crescendos through the air.

I get up, dusting off my blue jeans and shirt. To my left is a forest with a path. To my right is a giant "Start" sign coming out of the dirt. I reach out to touch the sign. It glimmers, fading as my fingers go through it, the pixels coming back together to form it once again.

I must have hit my head when I was trapped in the hall because there is no way that I've somehow managed to be inside a video game.

The strange little man appears in front of me, and I fall back onto my butt.

"Hello again! I'm Gorloc and this," he says cheerfully as he motions around with a dramatic wave of his hands, "is my gauntlet!"

I rub my temples. "I have to wake up. I have to wake up," I chant aloud.

Gorloc giggles. "My boy, you *are* awake."

"You mean to tell me that I got sucked into your game?"

"Of course! For your birthday, you get to play my gauntlet! Isn't that so much fun?" He claps his hands together with glee.

I haven't played a fantasy based video game in years. Not since games like *Call of Duty* and *Battlefield* made it onto the market.

"No, it is not *fun*! I want out of your game *now.*"

Gorloc's smile turns deadly serious. "Yes, Jonas, you can get out of here as soon as you finish the gauntlet and get the key."

I stand up and loom over Gorloc, digging my nails into my hands to keep myself from punching him. "What are you talking about?"

"For years, my gauntlet has been around, taking new warriors through different trials. Giving them a magic filled adventure, like Questland promises. Each warrior is different, as is each gauntlet." Gorloc rubs his hands together nervously. "Normally, the warriors are able to work through their strengths and weaknesses to find the key and win. In all of my years I've never seen anyone not conquer the gauntlet . . ."

"Gorloc, get to the point."

He looks at me sheepishly. "Well, the last chosen warrior never made it out. And while time works differently here compared to the real world, he's been here too long. It's up to you to find him and together you can retrieve the key!"

I shake my head. "I thought you had the key? This is your gauntlet. Why don't you get us out of here?"

"Oh, no, this is my gauntlet in name only. The gauntlet creates the rules and I cannot intervene. If you want to leave this place, you must find the other warrior and get the key."

This has to be the worst birthday gift ever. I may love video games, but I've never wanted to be *in* one. This is definitely going to be some adventure.

I look up at the hearts next to me. "What are those?" A nervous feeling enters my gut because if this is like any other video game—

"Those are your lives." Gorloc gulps.

I take a menacing step toward Gorloc. "And what exactly happens if I lose those?"

"Well, exactly what happened to the last warrior. You stay here until a new warrior is chosen."

The missing Questland kid . . .

"And how long does that take?"

"The timing for every warrior is different. The gauntlet chooses who it wants. But usually not long. Unless Questland gets shut down again . . . You must give one life to the lost warrior when you find him so that you can both leave the game."

There is no way I can lose these lives because I refuse to be stuck here for any longer than I have to be.

A drum begins to pound, shaking the ground as the "Start" sign blips out of existence.

"Well, enough jibber jabber. It's time to begin the gauntlet! Good luck, Jonas." Gorloc's figure dissipates and I'm left standing alone facing the path that leads into the forest.

The path through the forest is oddly quiet and incredibly boring. I whistle some tunes along my way. Either the gauntlet's trial is about me getting my steps in or this is the calm before the storm.

Speak of the devil.

Lightning spreads overhead as the trees begin to part. I'm led to a cliffside with the oldest bridge I've ever seen closing the gap. Smoke fills the air as heat rises and the smell of sulfur tickles my nose. I hate heights, but that doesn't stop my shaky legs from creeping to the edge of the cliff to look below. Beneath the bridge, many feet down, is a lake of fiery lava.

You have got *to be kidding me.*

Besides hating heights, one of my biggest fears is burning alive. I've heard that it's the worst death imaginable, and it's not something I ever want to experience. I especially don't want to experience burning in a fiery lake of lava.

Amidst the sky of smoke and lightning, a giant light pops up and a resounding *ding* echoes across the lake. In the sky are the words "The Trial of Courage."

So, the gauntlet knows two of my biggest fears. Well, it's a good thing that it only chose fire and heights because had it chosen . . .

A screech tears from above me as giant bats swoop and dive out of the smoke and over the bridge.

When I was younger, playing outside in our backyard, a bat came out of the tree and flew so low that it got tangled in my mess of black curls. It scratched and bit at my head while I flailed trying to get it free. It untangled itself and got away, but I ended up at the hospital receiving many rounds of rabies shots and a whole new phobia.

Terror gnaws at my insides as I take in their leathery wings and sharp fangs. The sound of them screeching makes my scalp itch. I can't get the image out of my head of bats trapped in my hair and biting me. My feet don't want to budge, and goosebumps sprout up my legs and inch up my arms.

But there's no other way out of this.

The only way forward is to cross the bridge, so I straighten my shoulders and place a tentative, quivering foot onto the first plank. The bridge of ropes and rotting wooden planks sways beneath me, creaking under my weight. The sound of flapping wings approaches. One bat swoops toward me. Its eyes hold a sinister glow. I quickly duck down to avoid it, feeling the rush of air as it passes over my head and heat from the churning lava below warms my face.

I have to keep moving.

I glance up to see that the bats are circling around and, taking a deep breath, I take my next few steps.

CRACK!

A weak plank beneath my foot crumbles, taking my leg along with it. Stumbling forward, I land hard against the bridge and a few more planks give way. I scramble to grab hold of another plank. Dangling above the lava, I feel the heat on the bottom of my tennis shoes.

I don't know what it'll feel like to lose a life in the gauntlet, and I really don't want to find out, but my grip isn't strong. There's no way I'll be able to pull myself up.

Think... Think...

This is the trial of courage, but maybe being courageous doesn't mean that I cross the bridge safely. Would that really make me courageous? Is it a true test of my courage if I manage to pull myself up and run away from my fears?

Maybe being courageous means taking a risk and facing my fears by embracing them.

A bat dives toward me. Its fangs protrude and it looks as if it's going to snap at my hands that are barely holding on.

Sucking in a breath and closing my eyes, I do the opposite of what my body wants me to do, and I let go, hoping that this works. Hoping that true courage is falling from a crazy height through bat infested territory into a lake of lava.

The movies always make it look so quick when the characters fall through the sky, but I seem to be falling forever. I start to wonder if my theory was right as I wait for the flames of the lava to lick across my body.

I open my eyes to see that I'm not falling at all. The bridge and bats aren't above me, and there's no lava below me. Instead, I'm in a dark cavern of sorts.

Trumpets blow from somewhere and confetti rains down from the ceiling. A green neon light appears in front of me. It says "Success!" in huge letters.

"Congratulations, Jonas! You passed the first trial!" Gorloc pops up beside me.

"Geez! You can't sneak up on a guy like that!" I kick him in the shin. He dramatically hops around on one leg.

"On to the next!" he shouts before disappearing.

"Thanks," I mumble.

The green neon light flickers away and I'm left in the pitch black, clueless.

How am I supposed to know what direction to go?

As if the gauntlet knows my thoughts, an orange glow appears ahead. I press my hand against the wall of the cavern as I make my way through the dark chamber toward the orange light.

The chamber leads me to a grand hall lit by torches and covered in books and scrolls from wall to wall. In the center of the hall is a giant statue holding a very large book and a sword. The domed ceiling is adorned by an intricate painting that reads "The Trial of Wisdom" in ornate letters.

Something shuffles in the darkness between one of the bookcases. I instantly go on edge, putting myself in a fighting stance in case I need to protect myself.

Out from the shadows comes a kid not much older than me, with blond scraggly hair and bloodshot green eyes. He's covered in dirt and a little bit of blood, but other than that he looks okay. Well, actually, maybe he looks a little less than okay, but at least he's alive.

"You the missing warrior?" I ask.

He nods and then clears his throat. "Sure am. My parents must be freaking by now. How long has it been out there? Like a week?"

Yikes. "Try a few months."

He curses. "Fabulous." He kicks a book across the floor.

"Is this the trial where you lost your lives?"

"I lost two of them here because I tried to aimlessly guess. Lost the third one on the last trial. I decided that this would be the safest place to come back to while I waited for the next warrior. At least I got to read to pass the time."

I reach up and pull one of my hearts down. "Here. I'm supposed to give you one of these."

He takes the heart with a huge grin. "Thanks!"

"Aren't you hungry? Thirsty?"

"No. Gorloc may not be able to intervene with the gauntlet, but he can bring food and drink while you're stuck here in purgatory."

"Purgatory? Seems like being stuck here would be more like Hell."

He scoffs. "You're not wrong."

"The name is Jonas, by the way." I stick my hand out to shake his.

"Eli."

I glance around the room. "So, what's the trial of wisdom?"

Eli shuffles toward the statue at the center of the room. "Approach the statue and answer the riddle correctly to get the Book of Wisdom."

"What the heck is the Book of Wisdom?" I quirk an eyebrow.

"The thing that will help you through your final trial." He shudders.

I'm afraid to ask my next question, but I need to know. "And what happens if I answer the riddle wrong?"

Eli stares at the statue, pointing a finger toward it. "See that sword?" He makes a slicing motion with his finger across his throat.

I nod, understanding. I'll be dead meat. "Can't you just tell me what the answer is?"

He shakes his head. "No can do. The gauntlet is different for every warrior, which means you have a different riddle and final trial."

I cluck my tongue. Perfect.

On shaky legs, I approach the statue. It groans to life, stone grinding together as its blank eyes stare into my own.

"Welcome, warrior," it says in a gravelly tone. Then, to my surprise, the statue begins to sing.

Lost within the depths of lore, where shadows and demons dwell
A creature stirs in dreams of gold, so all the legends tell.
With claws of steel, and heart aflame
Through ages past, it's been given a name.

Breath that turns the night to day,
A fearsome beast, the brave may sway.
Symbolic of both dread and awe
Yet, in the tombs, bound by law.
Written in tales of valor, fierce and bold,
This monster guards many treasures to behold.

The riddle ends, and now I can understand why Eli failed this trial more than once.

"How am I supposed to solve that?!"

Eli walks over to a table and begins to stack books in front of him. "The same way I solved mine. Read."

Oh, great, reading. I hate reading. I mean, I didn't used to hate it, but then video games entered my life. I haven't picked up a book since. It figures that the trial of wisdom wouldn't be something as simple as just solving a riddle. No, in order to have wisdom, you need to gain wisdom.

I plop down next to Eli and sift through a stack of books. "Okay, let's try and do this strategically so we're not just flipping through books that we don't actually need to flip through. Based on the parts where the riddle discusses legends, I'm going to say that this creature we're looking for is part of the fantasy genre."

"But what about the part that mentions demons dwelling? Wouldn't that say horror?" Eli has *Dracula* by Bram Stoker opened in front of him.

"Okay, there's two of us and two possible genres. Let's split up and make a list of possible creatures then we'll narrow it down from there."

I flip through various books from *Lord of the Rings* to *Alice's Adventures in Wonderland*, my eyes straining from looking over a bunch of words and pictures. The problem is that there are so many potential creatures it could be. After scanning many pages, I write things down like Jabberwock, Griffin, Dragon, and Basilisk.

A yawn escapes me. All this reading is exhausting. "What do you have?" I ask Eli.

He looks at his list. "Gargoyle, Hellhound, Cthulhu, and Chimera."

"All right. Our creature needs claws and a heart aflame, so fire breather?" There's a question in my voice, but I'm pretty confident.

"Definitely."

"Do you have a fire breather?"

"The chimera breathes fire." *Interesting.*

"All right, I have a dragon on my list. Which one do we go with?" This is where it could be tricky. Dragon seems like the obvious answer, but it's almost *too* obvious. I would think the trial of wisdom would want to be vague to create a true challenge.

"I have no idea. They both have legends written about them. They both breathe fire, and guard treasure. And in every story the chimera is viewed as fearsome."

"Well then let's go with that one!" Tired of sitting here with my nose in a book, I run up to the statue and give the answer before Eli can stop me. "The answer is chimera!" I shout with a smile.

The statue rumbles, the stone grinding as it shifts. Lifting the sword up, it stabs me straight through the stomach. I cry out, expecting to feel some sort of pain, but everything shimmers away into pixels and I'm plunged into darkness. A white light flashes in the darkness. It reads: "Respawn." I reach out and touch the light, and the world around me begins to spin.

I think I'm going to be sick.

The grand hall blips back into existence. Eli is still sitting at the table with a disappointed look on his face. "Welcome back," he says. "It's not a good idea to make a rushed decision during the trial of wisdom."

One of my hearts pops like a bubble. Only one left. Great.

"All right, so we go with the obvious then? Dragon?" I ask.

"The line, 'written in tales of valor, fierce and bold' would lead me to believe the answer is dragon and not chimera. Which is what I would have told you if you hadn't ran off to the statue." Eli crosses his arms, and I shrug.

Approaching the statue again, feeling like I may just pee my pants if this answer is wrong, I quietly say, "The answer is dragon," and wait with bated breath.

The statue begins its rumbling again, but this time the book in its hand cracks, the stone shriveling off it, and lands with a loud thud on the floor. The word "Success!" lights up the room.

Eli jumps up, slapping me on the back. "You did it!"

"No, *we* did it."

Eli grins and picks up the book to hand it to me.

The statue rotates to the right, opening up a hole in the ground with a staircase beneath it.

"Where do you think that leads?" My voice quivers.

"Probably to the final trial."

"Hip-Hip-Hooray!" Gorloc appears on the staircase. "You two used your brains and got through! One last trial and you'll be free!" He vanishes.

I huff out a breath. "When I can finally get my hands on that little guy . . ."

"You'll have to beat me to it," Eli concurs.

Together, like the two warriors we got thrust into being, we descend the stairs to meet our next trial. I open the book to see if I can get a head start on what the next trial may be. All the pages are blank except for one.

"You've got to be kidding me. This whole entire book, and only one page has words on it? What did your book have?" While I'm happy we don't have to read another book, I'd also like to have a little more guidance.

Eli looks over at the page. "My book had a map."

I read the page aloud. "In the keep that runs so deep, it lies restless and alone, waiting for a warrior to give back the golden Heartstone."

Eli rips the book from my hands, frantically turning the pages. "That's really all it says?!"

The staircase ends. We're led out into a lair filled with thousands and thousands of gemstones and twinkling golden treasures. Lit up like sparklers above us are the words "The Final Trial." Molten lava flows through the place and it creates a weird ambiance. The ground is incredibly uneven as Eli and I navigate around the treasures.

"What do you think we have to do?" I ask, squinting at the confusing rhyme on the page.

"I guess we look for the golden Heartstone." Eli walks toward a large pile of jewels.

If I thought that looking for the answer to a riddle in a book took forever, this was about to take an eternity. It is one ginormous vault. The torches on the sides of the cavernous room reflect off the gems. The air is thick with dust, and the whole place feels sticky and damp. My shirt clings to my body as I work my way through a pile of gems. I'm assuming that we'll know we've found it when Gorloc shows up or a key appears.

I hear coins and jewels clinking together as Eli frantically digs through his pile. His face is red with frustration. I don't blame him.

"You know for a final challenge, this sure could be a lot worse—"

A giant roar shakes the chamber, rattling the piles of treasures to the point of toppling over. A dragon, covered in silvery scales, flies over us, turning its head in every direction. Its wingspan must cover hundreds of feet and its tail is just as long with spikes protruding from the end. If it wasn't so terrifying, I'd be in awe at how majestic it is.

Eli races over to me as fast as he can and we hide ourselves behind a remaining pile of gems.

"You were freaking saying, Jonas?" Eli grits out.

The dragon roars again. An explosion rings, scattering gold in every direction as the dragon blasts out a ball of fire.

"What did you read about dragons?" Eli demands.

"What?"

Eli grabs my shoulders and stares into my eyes. "The trial of wisdom wouldn't have the answer to the riddle be dragon if it didn't think the information learned would be of value, right? Now, what did you read about dragons?"

Words flash across my mind as I try to recall anything I read—or skimmed—about dragons. Maybe I should have taken more time on that challenge than I did.

"Uh, they have wings, they breathe fire—"

Another fire bomb strikes from above, hitting a stack of gems way too close to us. We duck and cover.

"That's information we already know!" Eli hisses.

I start to rattle off information as quickly as I can. "They can have magical abilities, they're vindictive, but also protectors. And they're obsessed with hoarding the treasures they've earned." I glance around the vault. This dragon has clearly earned a lot.

"Anything on how to defeat one?" Eli asks, his voice a little shaky.

The dragon lands and causes the ground to quake.

"No. Not that it would matter because the only way to get out of this is to find the Heartstone," I whisper so the dragon won't hear us.

"Darn! Well, then I guess you better get to searching." Eli stands up and moves away from our hiding place.

I grab his arm. "Where the heck are you going?"

"I'm going to distract the dragon while you find that Heartstone. Do me a favor and don't take too long." Eli lets out a nervous laugh. He jumps out from behind the pile and waves his arms in the air. "Hey, dragon! Over here!"

The dragon bellows, whipping its tail around in anger and crashing into some gems. Eli takes off and the dragon follows in pursuit while I take the distraction to dig through treasures. My heart pounds with the added pressure of finding this stupid gem before Eli or I lose a life.

My eyes dart from one glittering thing to the next, holding it in my hand as I wait for some sort of sign that this may be the Heartstone. Each one gives me nothing, so I toss them behind me and move on to the next. I have to steady myself as I climb on top of the various piles, searching.

"Any day now, Jonas!" Eli says as he runs by. I duck down to hide myself from the dragon when it storms past. I watch atop my pile of jewels as the dragon spits out flames at Eli. He turns a corner quickly, narrowly missing the bite of the fire.

I grab a handful of golden gems and hold them up as though I'm offering them to the gauntlet as a sacrifice, praying that any one of them may be the Heartstone. Nothing. I toss the handful behind me in anger. Just then a shimmer catches my eye. The heart above me, the one keeping me in the game, reflects a golden hue as the flame from a torch on the wall hits it.

No.

There's no way that this is it.

"JONAS!" Eli screams.

But if I lose this heart, I lose the game. I'll be trapped just like Eli was. Who knows for how long? The heart shimmers again as if to mock me.

I think of the gauntlet and everything I've learned while being here. I faced my fears and won the trial of courage. I learned from my failure, and tested my knowledge to win the trial of wisdom. Maybe this final trial is set up this way so that I can put everything I've obtained to work. My brain is telling me that my final heart is the Heartstone that I need to give to the dragon. My fear is screaming at me, though, telling me if I give this up, I'm toast. But fear has a way of wriggling inside of me like an ugly worm, telling me there are things I'm incapable of when in my gut I know that I can do it. I can beat my fear. I can be courageous. I can willingly give this heart away and I won't lose because this isn't me dying, this is me thriving.

"HELP!" Eli screams again.

"I'm coming!" I yell back, racing toward Eli's frightened voice. He's trapped in a corner, the dragon slowly closing in on him, teeth bared, ready to devour him.

"Hey!" I shout. "I've got your Heartstone." I reach up and grab my heart. The ruby red that it used to be fades away, changing to a golden hue. The dragon's purple eyes light up.

I kneel before the dragon and present the Heartstone. As my heart beats like a drum in my chest, the dragon approaches me. It bows its head and gestures to the scales on its chest. There, in the center, is an empty, heart-shaped cavity. I gently walk toward the dragon, and reach up to click the Heartstone into place.

A key pops up next to me, and a burst of manic laughter escapes me.

I did it!

I jump up and grab the key, holding it tight.

The world around us goes static, the pixels all flitting away in a crazy storm. The dragon and all the jewels disintegrate into nothing as if they were never there to begin with. And then my body feels fuzzy. I look down at my hands to see that they're turning into whisps. They fade away with the rest of the video game.

I frantically look at Eli. To my relief, his body is doing the same thing and he looks just as weirded out and scared as I feel. Our bodies swirl and twirl together, a mixture of pixels and liquid in a blender.

Our screams follow us as we're spit out of the game and go tumbling out into the dark room where this birthday gift nightmare began. Getting our bearings, Eli and I take a moment to look at each other and just laugh. It's the most relieved I've ever felt in my entire life.

My relief is cut short, replaced by annoyance when I see Gorloc burst out of the game next to us.

"Congratulations, my friends!" He clicks his heels together as he hops in the air.

"If you think for one moment that we're friends . . ." Eli says through clenched teeth.

Eli and I step up to Gorloc, cornering him.

"Now, now, remember, the *gauntlet* chose you. I'm simply a pawn for its devices. And you can't be too mad at me. Didn't you learn lessons of great value?"

I gaze over at Eli and let out an exasperated sigh. "As much as I hate to admit it, I think we did learn some great lessons."

"Yeah, but I've been missing for months! How am I going to explain this all to my family? The police that have been looking for me!" Eli brings a fist toward Gorloc.

Gorloc waves his hands in front of him, stopping Eli before he can deck him. "It's all been erased! Everything is set right once again! It's a reward from the gauntlet. As far as your family knows, you've been at a birthday party for one of your friends all day." Gorloc winks. The little cretin. "Now, go enjoy the rest of the day! Questland awaits you." Gorloc snaps his fingers and he's gone.

When me and Eli emerge from the room that holds Gorloc's Gauntlet, we're greeted by my mom and dad.

"Oh, honey. We were wondering where you went off to," my mom says.

"Yeah, I just—" I turn to the room behind me. The door that was once a curtain is now the entrance to the men's restroom.

The magic of Questland.

"Needed to use the restroom after all that cake."

Eli nudges my side with a chuckle and I shrug my shoulders.

"Well, I think it's time for gifts, and then you boys can finish up with a few video games—"

"No!" Eli and I shout at the same time. My mom and dad give us a puzzled look.

I lower my voice back to a normal volume. "It's just, I think I'm video-gamed out for today. But maybe after presents we could go check out a bookstore."

"A bookstore? Jonas, you haven't read a book in ages." My mom raises her eyebrow.

I shrug. "What can I say, I've been itching to pick one up. Maybe something with dragons."

A Dragon's Gift

Austin D. Anderson

THE NIGHT MERRICK'S FATHER DIED remained an incomplete portrait in his mind. Parts of the memory showed in full color, unmistakably clear, while other details remained blank, or vaguely drawn. When he revisited the clear images, the emotions were still visceral. He could feel his father's icy hand in his again and see the blood running from claw gashes across his chest. The strongest man he had ever known strained as he lifted the blade into Merrick's hand. His labored word, a burden to carry thereafter: "Protect—"

Every time he held the sword from that moment on, the word returned like a phantom from the blade. Why had his father handed him the weapon? It was not the glassy, awestruck eyes, the gaping, breathless mouth, but the word that haunted him.

Protect.

Perhaps delirium had overtaken his father, or confusion about who he spoke to, but it seemed so direct, so personal. As the younger brother, why would he be charged with the role of protector? And protector of who, exactly? He could never be the guardian his father was for his family and his people. Yet five years later, the sword felt lighter than the night he received it. He ripped it free from the scabbard and cut through a line of imaginary foes. Perhaps, in time, he could become half the man his father was.

"Merrick," Kellan said with a not-so-subtle edge from the kitchen. Merrick placed the sword in the long chest beneath his bed and dashed towards the sound of his brother's voice.

A bevy of dismembered vegetables, chicken fat (and feathers), squash seeds, and spices laid on the table. The fire brought out every scent in the soup to full glory. Tender meat, carrots, and shaved onions cried out loudest from the boiling water, begging to be devoured. Kellan turned from his night's work and scowled at Merrick as hard as his mother used to.

"Did you enjoy your beauty rest?" Kellen said mirthlessly.

"I wasn't asleep. I—"

"I need you to go reposition Mother," Kellen said, before applying his finishing touches to the soup.

When Merrick entered his mother's room, he studied her subtle smile. He made his way to her bedside and took hold of her emaciated hand. Her appearance had worsened rapidly over the last few days. Even her golden hair had lost its usual sheen. With a heap of furs and blankets covering her, and the warmth permeating from the fireplace in the other room, she still looked winter-cold. As Merrick leaned closer, her pupils widened.

"My boy," she said, "you're growing by the day."

Merrick positioned his hand behind her back and sat her up. She felt no heavier than a bundle of twigs in his arms. Had he gained strength? Or had she lost more weight? Her collarbone hugged against skin and the shape of her face had narrowed, exposing a defined jawline. The pallidness of her skin accentuated the beautiful blue of her eyes. Even as the rest of her faded, her eyes held fast to life.

"You look just like him," she said, her voice dry.

His mother's words were like pendants adorned upon him. Yet resembling his father was not enough; he needed to match his feats of bravery, too. As he looked at his mother, it occurred to Merrick that he had spent the last several days talking about her to Kellen, Corani, and Garr, but he had not taken the time to talk to her. To simply enjoy her presence.

"I can't remember his face, only a shadow of it," Merrick said. He felt some shame in the confession, but five years is a long time, after all.

"Wait for a couple of years and look into a pool's reflection. You will see him there." She paused to breathe for a minute. "He had darker hair than yours, a bushy beard, but the same dark eyes."

Merrick could not find words, but he pondered his mother's. He felt like he could smile or cry, but he did neither. Something in him always caged those emotions. Now was no time to let them free.

"I know what those eyes mean," she said, with the biggest smile she could muster.

"What's that?" Merrick asked.

"Trouble. The bravest men always find trouble."

"I'll be . . . careful."

"Don't be careful, be clever," she said. "Stay a step ahead of all of us and no form of trouble will surprise you."

"I will," Merrick whispered, yet in that moment, his cleverness felt like a kitchen knife on the field of battle. What could wits do against a sickness far beyond his control? If it was a dreadful beast or army of brutes, he would have drawn his sword to fight, but what could he do against this? Anything would have been less of a horror than watching her suffer day after day with no way to help.

He turned to the doorway as Kellan brought in a steaming bowl and water pitcher.

"You are too good to me," Mother said.

"Go on, try it," Kellan said, dodging the affirmation.

"Kellan, you're getting quite good at this. Much better than your father ever was." She kissed Kellan's hand in thanks, and his cheeks grew red as he cracked half a grin, more mirth than he had shown in weeks. Kellan always jumped from one task to the next and never had trouble letting Merrick know what chores needed to be done. Merrick always appreciated the moments when he slowed down, even briefly.

"Go on. Serve some to your brother. We can have family dinner here. We don't need a table."

Merrick was only a couple of bites in when a knock sounded on the wooden door.

"It's Garr and Corani," Mother said. "I need you two to stay by the fire for a while. Corani needs to check on me."

Kellan lost some color in his cheeks as his characteristically sullen expression returned.

"She's . . . going to check if I'm getting any better. Lucky for you two, the best storyteller south of Alcos will be with you."

Kellan kissed her forehead and departed. Merrick lingered for a moment beside his mother. He felt a strange urge to apologize to her, but had done nothing wrong. Looking at her sickly features, his soul burned to make this right, but how? He felt her cool skin as he wrapped his arms around her and took one last look at the fight in her eyes. Desperation bubbled up in him as he considered her words: "Don't be careful, be clever."

Merrick watched the flames slowly devour each piece of timber. Garr was halfway through a story about the hidden city of Alcane, but Merrick had missed most of it. He had heard it all before, and there were more pressing matters at hand.

When Garr concluded, a long silence filled the room, and Merrick took his opportunity. "The stories of the hoard of treasure in the heart of Alcane, are they true?" Merrick asked, turning towards Garr.

The fire danced across Garr's wide, black eyes as he cleared his throat. "There are many stories of the hoard," Garr said, his throaty voice echoing through the quiet room. Garr's voice had the rhythm of a minstrel, even without the accompaniment of strings. The wildness of his sound could immerse anyone in tales of adventure, except for Merrick on this night. Instead, he studied the scar snaking from the side of his neck up to his lips. "The dragoness guards those spoils of men," Garr continued.

"Is it true?" Merrick asked, gritting his teeth. He didn't need some childhood story. He needed answers.

"If it's the truth you want, I can give my best go at it," Garr said, "but the darker parts may linger in your minds, especially when the moon is high."

Kellan edged forward in his seat. "I'm sure we can handle it," he said without hesitation.

"Very well," Garr said. "You are the children of Horick, after all, and young men at that."

Rain pounded on the thatch and wind crept through gaps in the walls as Garr repositioned himself. The orange gleam fell on him, revealing an empty sleeve on his left side (the same side as the scars).

"Alcane was not always a den of bones and ruin. It was once a trade city for folks as far south as Salgos. Legend states that the dragoness, from the stone lands to the north, took the shape of a woman. A form as radiant as any queen or fair maiden. She appeared before King Aldain to negotiate a peace between his people and her kind."

Merrick fought the impulse to interject. Garr rarely spared a detail, especially when the fire burned hot and listening ears surrounded him. He cleared his throat and continued.

"The dragoness brought with her a peace offering, a gift for Aldain's people."

"Dragon's milk," Merrick interrupted.

"Yes, that is what men came to call it. Yet the simple term cannot do justice to the thing itself. A substance created by her own body, unique to the fur-dragons of the north. Surely, she used it to nourish her young ones, but to call it milk is like calling an oak tree a dandelion. Yet men have their ways of simplifying things."

Merrick looked away from the fire and found himself

inching towards Garr, eager for the next words.

"It is said the substance can cure any ailment of human—or even animal—kind. As a mother's breast milk can cure sickness of the child, or even mend cuts and bruises, so too can dragon's milk heal. When King Aldain discovered this secret, his city prospered. Trade increased with outsiders and the wealth of the city overflowed. As the peace continued between dragons and men, the dragoness continued to provide her gifts. Fine craftsmen paid tribute to her with eloquent masonry and architecture. None more notable than King Aldain's Hall. There, he and his men lorded over the hoards of treasure from distant lands and the precious source of their prosperity."

Garr stared contemplatively into the fire. He took a deep breath, seemingly reluctant to share the next words.

"Yet the men and women of Alcane had made a deadly mistake: trusting a dragon. After years of industry and peace, all progress came to an end one dreadful night. The dragoness descended from the peaks. Black as a stallion in the twilight, she entered the king's domain. Purple fire engulfed the hall, magic flames not merely of destruction, but of special purpose. Every soldier caught in her fire became a corpse in an instant, without a trace of flesh to be discovered. Those majestic halls remained unscathed, but everyone inside became a collection of ivory. A dragon loves nothing more than a hoard of precious treasures, and Aldain had given her just that. Some say the crown still sits upon his aged bones."

"What of the treasure?" Merrick asked.

"It remains in the center of the desolate city to this day, in the hall of the king." Garr said. "In all of her cunning, the dragoness dwells with it. The chief end of her schemes. As for the bones of the Alcanians, her purple flames awoke them into cruel amalgamations. Dry bones remade into something else, something dreadful—oskoll."

Garr practically whispered the word. The way it rolled off his tongue sounded like a dark enchantment. Merrick felt a trimmer run down his hand, and soon he found himself picking at his nails. Suddenly, the flapping shutters and bellows of the wind became more poignant. Even from Garr's smooth, deep voice, the word sounded unnatural.

"The oskoll are thoughtless, guided only by the will of the dragoness. They protect the hoard at all costs," Garr added.

"In the last stand with father, did you see the hoard?" Merrick asked.

"No . . . our encounter with the beast was in the city's south end, but an Alcanian soldier in our company swore he had seen the treasure with his own eyes. Floods of gold, emerald, even scarce vials of dragon's milk. He claimed to have escaped narrowly, with the ancient sword of Aldain himself. Yet the sword was not enough to grant us victory. The dragoness rampaged our garrison and drove the remnant of Alcanians through the gorge and into the farmlands. And only a fool would enter the city again."

"Well, that is quite a story to be telling to young ones." Corani said from the hallway. Like Garr, her voice had a power, but of a different kind. It soothed with a gentler melody. There is no broken heart or damaged spirit it could not mend. She spoke this way to everyone, but especially to mother.

Garr flushed, a strange sight to behold, then stumbled over his next few words. "Yes, and it is late, after all. More stories for another day, I suppose."

"We should be on our way, but I will be back in the morning." Corani said, wrapping herself in a coat of furs. Before she and Garr could leave, Kellan stopped them at the door to have a private conversation. Merrick stayed by the hearth, staring deep into the flames, mulling over Garr's words.

Merrick shook his brother's shoulder once more. This time, Kellan shot up as if oskoll terrorized his dreams. After a couple of long breaths, he turned to his brother. "Is everything alright?"

"How long does she have?" Merrick asked before a second could pass.

"Days," Kellan replied, rubbing sleep from his eyes. "There's nothing we can do for her."

Kellan's eyes fell on the floor as if speaking those words aloud had somehow made them real.

"What if we could do something?" Merrick asked.

"You've got that look about you, brother."

"What look?" Merrick asked, incredulously.

"It's the look you make before saying something foolish."

"Hear me out . . . I know my ideas haven't always panned out, but we have no other options."

Kellan nodded begrudgingly. "Go on."

"I cannot stop thinking about what Garr said. About the Alcanian soldier. I know it's a long shot, but what if there truly is dragon's milk tucked away in Aldain's Hall? What if—"

"And what of the dragoness? At what stage of your plan does she burn us to bones?"

"Of course there would be risks, but I cannot sit here while Mother—" Merrick stopped himself as he felt tears welling in his eyes.

"I know how hard this is for you," Kellan said, slipping his arm around Merrick's shoulder. "But you're better off here with us than dead in the Way of Bones."

"I won't stay here. Father asked me. He said—"

"You think you can best the very dragon that ended him?"

"I don't know, but I have to try."

"Merrick, please."

"I can get into the hall unseen. You know I am light on my feet. At dawn I'm leaving, with or without you." Merrick stood and let his brother's arm drop behind him. Tears blurred his vision as he walked through the door, and he muttered again, "I have to try."

The sword hung awkwardly at his side. Its weight pulled his body to the left like a broken rudder, the edge reaching nearly to the ground. The pack on his back offset it just enough to keep him on his feet. Merrick paused, repositioned, and glanced back toward home. Mist danced over the barren soil plots and inside of the makeshift goat pins. Even the animals were asleep, creating a deathly silence. He looked at the faded wood siding, the thatch he had helped Garr replace last spring, and the smoke cloud from the chimney as it disappeared into the murky sky.

He pushed down on the hilt to balance the sword as much as he could.

"This is the only way," Merrick whispered to himself. He longed, from deep in his soul, to hear his father interject from clouds or in the wind. The details of his face were gone, but he still remembered the sound of his voice, equal parts loving and firm. He needed to hear it now, yet he knew he never would again. A tear warmed his cool cheek as father's last word returned like a throbbing bruise.

"Merrick."

The voice, no more than a whisper, came from the direction of the house.

Kellan approached, wearing a black wool tunic with a walking stick in hand. Merrick looked up at his brother, bracing himself for another lecture.

"Stupid idea or not . . . you're not going alone," Kellan said as he got closer.

"A fool's plan is better than no plan at all." Merrick felt his lips stretch into a grin. "What about Mother?"

"Mother is asleep, warm in her bed. Corani will be back shortly to check on her. I wrote her a note letting her know we are drawing water from the well, which we will . . . once we've accomplished the task."

After a few miles of farmlands, they reached a broader road, an ancient way to Alcane. As the land grew rocky, a man passed beside them in tattered clothing. He reeked worse than dead vermin, and his wild hair jetted on both sides of his head. With widened pupils, he looked Merrick dead in the eyes, and said, "Fear. Fear the Way of Bones. Where the dead walk and the living die."

A chill ran across Merrick's skin, awaking all of his senses. It's one thing to hear about a place one hundred times, experiencing it is something else entirely. Kellan urged him to keep moving. The words echoed in Merrick's mind long after the man vanished from view.

No markers remained on the old trade route. All was vacant, aside from the dismembered parts of an old wagon. Even the stones looked sickly pale, surrounded by withered weeds and scarce dirt. Merrick breathed the stagnant air and suddenly felt drowsy.

They walked for hours, but they seemed to make no progress. Without milestones to account for, the rows of stone looked identical. An unsettling silence overpowered every other detail of the Way as if all traces of life had been drained there by unnatural means. Kellan froze, shielding Merrick from going forward.

A cadaverous hand emerged from a chasm in the rock, awoken from death itself.

Merrick could hardly believe his eyes as its body followed from a wild crypt. He spoke the accursed word aloud, for the first time: "Oskoll."

A walking skeleton, even worse than the stories, stood before them. Merrick felt cold sweat run across his palms as he looked up at it. On top of its neck rested a grotesque skull. Unlike the rest of its body, the skull was not a man's; it had an elongated snout with sharpened fangs. Merrick's hand trembled as he reached for the hilt of his sword. As it neared them, its teeth grated together crudely, an unbearable sound. It honed in on them by some dark magic that had bound its bones together. Raising a makeshift mace, it hurtled in their direction.

Kellan clutched his staff with two hands. Merrick moved aside and yanked on the hilt, but the blade remained lodged in the scabbard. With as much strength as he could muster, he pulled until the sword flung free and out of his hand, clanking into a nearby boulder. Merrick stooped to retrieve it as Kellan dealt the first blow. A crack of wood and ivory echoed down the gorge. The oskoll staggered but kept its balance by grabbing Kellan's weapon. Ripping it free from his hand with its left arm, it soon raised its mace again.

Merrick swung the sword, guided by adrenaline-fueled instinct. Steel connected with its neck bone, and the skull clanked free against rough dirt. Pausing only for a moment, the oskoll's skeletal arm swung towards its target. Kellan dove to the side as the weapon dented the ground. The headless brute swung wildly as Kellan rolled across the dirt. Merrick charged again with his sword, but with a swift swing, the oskoll batted the blade out of his hand.

As Merrick regained his footing, something whirled through the air in front of him. It collided with the oskoll's right arm, sending the mace in a spin through the air. Soon, a second axe took off the other arm. Merrick retrieved his swords and sliced through its midsection, leaving a collection of scattered bones on the ground.

"We need to move," a voice bellowed from behind them.

Kellan scrambled to his feet, and Merrick retrieved one of the axes, reaching his arm toward the newcomer.

"Move," Garr said, holstering the first axe and grabbing the second from the ground.

Merrick gasped for air as he tried to keep up with Garr and Kellan. Garr had led them to an incision in the rock wall, just wide enough for the three of them. He handed Merrick his waterskin. Two quick swigs brought back his vigor.

After the three were hydrated, Kellan interrupted a prolonged silence. "Aren't you going to tell us to go back?"

"You are Horick's children, are you not? I'd be wasting my breath," Garr said. "You have made your choice. Now, we see it through."

Merrick intended to. He knew what needed to be done. His whole body pulsated in exhilaration at the words. "Like you and Father did." Merrick's attention drifted to the armor Garr wore. His chest plate and arm guards made him look far younger. The left shoulder of the armor had harsh edges, a noticeable blemish on otherwise immaculate panoply. "Did you wear this very armor when you two were here?" Merrick asked.

"Yes, and I have been praying for the right cause to put it on again," Garr said, his mind somewhere far off. "I owe it to your father after what he did for me. I would have died, along with the entire garrison, had he not stood against the beast alone. Had I been stronger, maybe I—"

"Nonsense," Kellan said, his arm on Garr's good shoulder.

Garr rarely spoke about the day their father died, and when he did, his voice often sounded strained as if speaking the words brought about a special pain in him. Garr's deep, melodic voice returned as he changed the subject.

"Right . . . what's important now is dragon's milk. I could

see it in both of your eyes last night. You believe it is more than a story, and you are right."

"How far are we from the city?" Merrick asked.

"Two to three more miles, I'd wager. We'll need to stay light on our feet. Night is not far away and there will be oskoll about. I imagine our friend back there was once under the influence of the dragoness, but wandered off on its own. We will face sharper foes in Alcane, swords under her direct will."

"Unless we can make it to the hall unseen," Merrick said.

"A task all but impossible," Garr replied. "We ne—" Garr sniffed the air and followed a scent like a hunter's hound. "She's close, and she's been feeding," Garr murmured as he moved further down the gorge.

Merrick and Kellan followed, and each step drew them closer to a rancid scent. By the time they reached the dark heap, Merrick retched at the smell. Garr opened a leather pack at his side and knelt near the dung pile. Kellan raised his eyebrows at Merrick incredulously. Merrick tried to keep his breakfast down as he Garr grabbed a handful of the filth and secured it in his pack.

"A day or two old," Garr said. "She had a feast on something big. They say she prefers predators for feeding, bears and wolves. She must prove to the wild that she is the highest hunter, the top of the chain."

"Why on earth are you keeping that?" Kellan interjected.

"I am a farmer, my boy, and dragon's muck is our long-kept secret. Even a small drop, mixed into good soil, can enliven acres of crops and revitalize gardens for years. Our fields will be plentiful again." Garr stooped down to wash his hand in a shallow puddle. He then ran ahead, urging Merrick and Kellan to follow. "Dragons offer many gifts. Some are more strange than others." Garr cracked half a smile.

Merrick hugged the edge of the gorge as they jogged behind Garr, inching closer and closer to the city. Merrick's senses remained heightened. The haze in the air strained his lungs and hid the secret tunnels of the Way.

A voice interrupted the silence, jolting the company to a stop. Garr drew his axe.

"Well, well, what do we have here?" A woman's voice echoed from a shadowy cavern near them. Her voice sounded gravelly, perhaps even strained by an injured throat. She emerged from the shadows, gaunt as a starved wolf. A mask covered her facial features except for her deepset green eyes. Her tunic had many tears, and the wind blew at the edges of its loose fabric. Beside her, two hulking men wore similar dark, tattered garments, armed with long daggers. "No one enters the Way of Bones without cause," she said. "Ulf will want to know theirs. Bind them and take them to camp."

"Yes, Lady Lirael," the men replied.

Merrick reached for his sword, but Garr's hand clamped down on his. Garr raised his arm out to be tied, and Merrick and Kellan followed behind him.

"We found them snooping around in the Way," Lirael said to a man near the fire at the edge of their encampment. Smoke rose in front of him towards a high ceiling of the cave.

He took a swig of his canteen but said nothing. With the flick of two of his fingers, the men led Merrick and Kellan closer and pushed them to their knees. The rough stone broke through Merrick's trousers, scraping his skin. A sharp pain followed, but he gave little thought to it. He fixed his gaze instead on the aged face, dark eyes, and a long black beard exposed by fire light. The fine hairs on his arms threatened to jump off his skin. As Garr knelt beside him, Merrick breathed a little easier, but the fear still pounded at his heart.

"You must be foolish as us to be here at nightfall," the voice grumbled, deep as a bear. He moved from the fire to get a better look. Hunching over, he inspected Kellan then Merrick and chuckled mirthlessly. "Young pups."

"Pups with a good cause," Garr said.

"I don't forget a voice," the burly man replied. "If it isn't old Garr. Fancy meeting you back in the Way. You've one less arm than last we met." The man chuckled again, but the sound felt wrong in a place so dark and cursed. Merrick's stomach turned.

"Ulf." Garr nodded at the man before adding, "You've earned some new scars yourself."

Merrick studied a discolored wound running from the man's forehead down to his mustache.

"What is your purpose here?"

"These are Horick's boys. Their mother is in a bad way. They—"

"We're after dragon's milk, and nothing more," Merrick interrupted.

"Ah, how noble. Perhaps you truly are his sons." Ulf spat onto the stones beside Merrick and raised his chin for one more examination. "Hmm . . . Yes, I can see it. When the night darkens, we will raid the hall, take what we can, and if all goes well, put an end to the fork-tongued witch. Does that sound like a quest for a child?"

"I suppose not," Garr said. "But what harm would it be, if along the way, I retrieved the vial for them?"

"No trouble, far as I'm concerned." Ulf snorted. "But the children stay behind. I can't have them running amuck, disturbing the dragoness."

"As you wish, but they won't be harmed."

"Give us your aid, and they shall remain here with some of my men. I am indebted to Horick as you are."

Ulf nursed the canteen and motioned towards a corner of the cave behind the fire. The masked woman and one of Ulf's men walked Merrick and Kellan to a post near a rock wall. They fashioned a knot in the rope to secure them to two neighboring posts.

"What of my sword, Lirael?" Merrick asked.

She stooped to his level and pulled her mask down, revealing a gaunt, grime-covered face.

"I will watch over it myself, young one. It is no small thing that you are doing for your mother. I know it seems wrong, but you are better off here for now. You know, I lost my sons in all this madness. You remind me of them. The fire in you both is not easily quenched."

Before Merrick could offer his condolences, she slung the scabbard over her shoulder and disappeared into a line of soldiers beyond the fire.

"She's right, you know," Kellan said from beside him. The two sat shoulder to shoulder on the unforgiving ground. "Garr is our best shot at getting a vial. Perhaps we will return home in one piece, after all."

"We're not boys, like they keep saying," Merrick said. "And what happened to your staff?"

"It's useless now. It nearly cracked in two against that . . . thing. Not all of us have a fancy sword for protection."

"I—" Merrick stuttered.

"It's all right. I used to wonder why he placed it in your hand, but seeing you wield it today, well, I understand. You're a fighter, brother. He knew it. No matter how brazen and foolish you are at times, you have his spirit in you."

"I still wonder why he gave it to me. When his wiser son stood near."

A five-year wall dissipated between them at that moment. Merrick could finally speak freely about the memory that held his mind captive day after day.

"His wiser son never would have dreamed of coming this far, even if it needed to be done," Kellan added.

Merrick felt light, even free, as if a deadweight had fallen from his shoulders. He repositioned himself, moving as close to Kellan as the restraints allowed him. "You're a good brother. Father would be proud of all you've done for me . . . for Mother."

After a brief silence, Kellan changed the subject. As always, he dodged the kind words. "What's our next move?"

Merrick's eyes wandered throughout the cave to scarce pockets of torch light. He counted about thirty men in total and two or three women. The group could not have been of a single tribe. Some men bore the accents of southerners, others looked more like farmers than warriors, and a few men even bore Alcanian mail and armor. It seemed several clans had all rallied together for a similar cause under Ulf.

Suddenly, two soldiers ran into the cave, breathing steam

through the frigid air.

"The dragoness is at our heels, a garrison of oskoll. Draw your swords! The walking bones are upon us."

A crude mixture of voices and shuffling boots filled the cave. Two men near the entry fell backwards and cadaverous shadows stretched across the cave wall near the campfire. Rhythmic clanks of metal and ivory deafened Merricks ears. Garr was among the fighters with his axe in hand.

As oskoll breached like a broken dam, Merrick shivered at the purple light emanating from where their eyes should have been. Some had the skulls of men, others the skulls of misshapen beasts. All his nightmares had come to life. The army moved with the efficiency of the living. Men fell and bellowed, bow strings quivered, creating a din of indistinguishable chaos. Merrick's heart throbbed. He fought the restraint, but to no avail. He was tied bait for hungry sharks. Desperation boiled as he tugged on the rope again. Out of the corner of his eye, a soldier flew through the air and over the fire. The man's helmet came free and hurled closer and closer until it clanked off Merrick's forehead. A sharp pain followed before everything went black.

Merrick awoke under the moon's radiance. The ropes binding his wrists had rubbed the skin raw. His head throbbed as memories from the cave returned in fragments. Where was he now?

"Thank God you're awake," Kellan said from beside him. "I was starting to worry."

He turned towards his brother as the wood paneling beneath them started to move. Merrick nearly let out a yelp as he realized what surrounded them. An army of walking bones in Alcanian armor led the open carriage through the city street. The skeletons of two horses hauled the carriage, purple lanterns glowing in their eye sockets. Merrick hoped to wake up from the strange fever dream, yet there was no escape. Shadows hid most of the city now, but he took note of the ruins of buildings, broken stonework, and lightless homes. They must have been growing close to the city's center, to Aldain's Hall.

Across from Merrick, two others were bound. Garr's arm was tied to a metal bar in the interior, and Lirael sat beside him, arms secured behind her back. Bandages covered her neck and shoulder, a dark stripe showed through the gauze.

"What happened to all the others?" Merrick whispered.

"Dead," Lirael interjected. "All of them."

"Why have we been left alive?" Kellan asked discreetly.

"Do not seek to understand the mind of a dragon. It is beyond you, boy," Lirael said, wincing in pain.

The army of the dragoness marched in perfect unison beside them. Merrick found his eyes wandering from soldier to soldier to observe each one. Most of the oskoll were composed of the bones of men, but one near the carriage had a wolf's skull atop its human cadaver, and another towered over the others with what looked like a bear's elongated skeleton. It seemed the dragoness had crudely grafted some of her soldiers with new ivory parts, but all bore her purple markers as eyes. Merrick shuttered at her dark art, her unnatural creations. The carriage slowed as the oskoll reached their destination.

Even in the dark, Aldain's Hall was a sight to behold.

Pillars stood wider than farm homes in the foyer. Dragon statues stretched toward the broad ceiling. Purple banners fluttered above bearing the sigil of Aldain, and the exterior door stood in extravagance, wide enough for the carriage to enter. As if on cue, two oskoll drew open the chamber's entry. Purple light flooded into the night, inviting the party inside. Merrick's heart sunk in a strange mix of terror and wonder.

Torches hung on every level, emanating the light of the dragoness. Even the fire pits radiated hues of violet as opposed to normal flames. The logs within looked unscathed, yet the fires burned all the same. On the other side of the barren room, the floor was lofted with a throne set in the center. Behind it, a multitude of treasures led to a closed storeroom. As vast as it was, Merrick knew only a remnant of the cache was before them. A crowned skeleton sat prominently upon the throne above all the spoils.

One of the soldiers grabbed Merrick by the back of the neck with its bony, chilled fingers. After tossing him to the ground, it did the same to Kellan and Lirael. Another oskoll held a chain connected to the restraint at Garr's wrist and led him near the others like a captured hound. Two other soldiers threw Merrick's sword, a whole collection of daggers, and Garr's axes and belongings just out of reach of the group. One of the oskoll, with a golden helm bearing the symbol of Aldain, turned to the king. His jaws opened and glowed purple as it spoke in a harsh, dark language. The king spoke something back, and he rose from his throne, then all but a few of the oskoll departed.

As the king stood, he drew his blade and gnashed his teeth. He wore all the garments of a royalty, but they were tattered and aged. His crown, however, looked brand new. As he descended the stairs, Garr grabbed hold of the fastened chain and pulled with all his might. The skeletal arms securing him ripped free from the oskoll's body. Then, Garr dove toward one of his axes. Securing the weapon, he charged Aldain with a cry to make a bear cower, but before the two could reach each other, Lirael stood and yelled toward the king, "Sit down, you big oaf!"

His purple fire gleamed all the brighter. Loosening his posture, he dropped the sword, letting it clank down the stairs, and returned to his throne. He soon grew limp and colorless, like an ordinary skeleton.

"That one really has a mind of its own," Lirael said, as the rope on her hands vanished into purple flames. The ropes binding Merrick and Kellan vanished as well.

Before their eyes, her form changed from a grungy warrior into a dark-haired, fair maiden with all the elegance of a queen. She wore a radiant violet gown, and a crown materialized atop her head. No signs of the wound from the oskoll remained on her neck. She walked with refined dignity to Horick's sword on the ground and used it to cut the restraints of Kellan first, then Merrick. Garr tightened his grip on the axe until his hand went pale.

"Boy, as I said, I will hold on to the sword. I can smell my blood on it, a rare scent. I'm sure you know the power that can bring," the dragoness said, her eyes burning into him. "You are good-hearted boys, but even the kindest young men grow corrupt with age. Your kind is all the same."

Merrick's empty hands trembled, defenseless without his father's blade. The words he wanted to say were stuck to his tongue . . . It was really her.

"What do dragons know of the heart?" He stammered, evoking a worried glance from Kellan. "Are you not the one who betrayed Aldain? And for what, a hoard of riches?"

She laughed, a sickly blend of mirth and horror. "Is that the story men have passed down? I shouldn't be surprised. I'm sure it's merely by accident that they omitted the part when Aldain, and his men, murdered my two sons to line their own pockets and put their minds at ease. My boys were right to assume the worst of men. They withheld their trust, as I should have."

"Lies," Garr said. "You deceived Aldain, deceived us all."

"Well, of course I did," she said in an even tone. "After he deceived me."

"Don't listen to her," Garr said, turning his head.

"We could argue all night about the past, but it appears you have pressing matters to attend to." She walked towards Merrick and leaned in so close he could feel her hot breath on his skin.

"Dragon's milk," he said, avoiding looking into her eyes.

She craned her thin neck into his line of sight until he had no choice but to study the purple rings around her otherwise black irises.

"Yes," she said. "The reason you came all this way . . . A child's love is a powerful thing. I knew there was something about you both, something different. Unfortunately, there is a cost for what you seek. You see, without babies to feed and nurture, my body no longer creates it. Lucky for you both, however, there are some vials here."

"What's the cost?" Merrick said.

"Straight to the point. I like that about you," she said with a contemplative sigh. "The cost for a vial of life is . . . life. And—"

"I'll do it," Kellan said before Merrick could process her words.

"Ah. Just like a firstborn to be so noble." She said with a beautifully twisted smile.

"Show us the vial first," Garr growled back.

"Of course, of course."

She pulled out a finger-thin glass filled with an indigo substance. It felt as real as the bruise on his head as she placed it into Merrick's hand. The dragoness leaned in, uncomfortably close and whispered: "But know this, if you take a single step before the price is paid, I'll flood this entire hall with my fire."

Terror coursed through Merricks veins as he clutched the vial and gritted his teeth.

"Where are my manners? You will have to forgive me. I'm not dressed for the occasion." The dragoness's slim neck grew along with her perfect white teeth, and her face became something like a snout. Claws emerged from her fingers, and wild purple fire burned in her eyes. Garr turned toward Kellan, placing his axe into his hand, along with his pack of dragon's muck.

"Your father would be proud of the men you have become," Garr said, his eyes welling. "Let me repay him tonight. Life for life."

Merrick could not look away from the dragoness in her full and terrible form. She lurched over Garr as he walked to the center of the hall. Her horrible laugh echoed off of the walls as she admired him. Fur as short and sheen as a dark horse covered her body. Her wings extended nearly from wall to wall as she opened her mouth and unleashed a blaze of purple fire. Garr did not cower or attempt to flee. He remained statue-still in spite of the engulfing flames. Even his bones stood bold and defiant for a moment before toppling to the ground.

Merrick felt Kellan's firm hand around his trembling wrist. As they turned and ran, Merrick felt a gust of heat at their backs.

The run from Alcane to the edge of the Way was blurred by pure adrenaline. Merrick did not notice his level of exhaustion until he nearly toppled into the community well at the edge of the farmlands. As he and Kellan guzzled water, his thoughts were singular. Mother needed him. He pictured her confined in bed, devoid of color, and mustered the strength to keep moving. Kellan ran beside him, axe in hand. The morning light revealed tear stains on his filthy face.

The warmth of the dragoness's fire returned to his memory along with the haunting image of Garr's flesh fading to nothing, but his bones standing strong, unyielding. Suddenly, Merrick felt sick to his stomach. Garr was gone, just like Father, but now was not the time to mourn him. He owed it to Garr, just as much as Mother, to keep running. A new wave of energy met him near the Atwell farms, when he knew they were nearing home.

The clucks of chicken and bleats of goats welcomed them. The commotion of noise and flying feathers brought Corani from Mother's room to the doorway. Merrick's heart throbbed in his chest. His mother was mere steps away.

"You both had better come inside," Corani said from the threshold. Before Merrick entered, he saw Kellan lead her outside by the hand, and it wasn't long before he heard her muffled sobs—an unnerving sound coming from a spirit as sweet as hers. Desperation compelled Merrick forward with the vial tight in hand.

His mother's eyes were half-closed when he took a seat beside the bed. She opened her mouth and tried to speak, but only a bit of air escaped.

"Mother . . . Kellan and I, we—"

"I know," she said, in a rasp. "You found trouble." Her eyes were fully shut by the time she finished speaking. She muttered something about seeing his father far beyond the mountains, where the sun never sets.

"Horick," Mother whispered, as if Father were in the room.

"Will you drink it, Mother? Please?" Tears blurred his vision.

"Drink—" she murmured, with a subtle nod.

More color had drained from her. She looked like a pallid shell of her past self. Merrick raised the vial to her lips and gently poured the dragon's milk down her throat. As he watched the final drops disappear from the glass, he leaned in to check her pulse, as Corani had taught him. It was still beating, but weakening.

She looked devoid of life, motionless, with her eyes closed. Merrick inspected her lungs as they rose and fell, ever-so-slowly.

It wasn't working. More tears rolled down his cheeks. Was he too late? Did the dragoness give them enough in the vial? And Garr . . . did he die for nothing? In that moment, all the emotions he had kept at bay broke through the dam of his heart and rushed out. Merrick buried his mud-covered face in the clean-white blanket and sobbed.

The engulfing purple fire flooded his mind. He wept for Garr's brave bones and for the mother he once knew. With Father's sword miles away, he could not shake the weight of his failure. What else could he do now but weep?

A soft hand on his back jarred him. He turned his head, rubbing snot and mud from above his lips.

"I'm here, brother," Kellan said.

"It didn't work." Merrick stuttered over his words.

Kellan set Garr's axe on the foot of the bed, kneeled beside Merrick, and wrapped his arm around him. "No, not yet. Give it time," Kellan said. "Garr believed in this remedy enough to give his life for it. We will wait here until the dragon's milk does its work."

Merrick laid beside his mother, wrapping her frigid fingers in his. Kellan sat in the chair near him, and together they waited, fighting soft sobs.

Merrick freed his hand from the soil and wiped it clean. Almost immediately, more sweat ran down his arms, mixing with the grime on his skin. The summer illuminated green hills and miles of patterned crop lines to the south. Corani and Kellan labored with him, adding tulips to the edge of the garden plot.

Regardless of their proper season, flowers bloomed, fruits ripened, and vegetables reached full health. Bees scuttled amongst the plantings, and choirs of birds filled the nearest trees.

Beyond the acres teeming with life, Merrick spotted his mother.

Her golden hair flew unrestrained in the wind as she approached with two pots full of daisies, a rainbow of color in each hand. Merrick could not decide if she had always been so beautiful, or if the dragon's milk had provided a new radiance. Either way, as she neared, smiling ear to ear at their work, Merrick could hardly believe his eyes. She walked with the dignity of a queen over a wild countryside.

As Merrick watched her kneel beside Corani to add flowers to the last of the soil enriched by dragon's muck, the final word of his father made sense, at last. He knew his mother would protect Corani until the end of her days, just as Garr had protected all of them.

Kellan arose from his toil with Garr's axe hanging at his side. For now, it proved useful for felling small trees and cutting overgrowth. When his eyes met Merrick, he offered an approving nod and a contagious smile.

"The axe suits you," Merrick said.

"You think so?" Kellan asked. "Perhaps a day will come when I will put it to proper use."

"On that day, I will be by your side. As you were by mine," Merrick replied. "Thank you, for going along with a fool's plan."

Kellan wrapped his arm around Merrick and motioned towards Mother. "She's alive because of your plan, brother. If you're a fool, then I am, too. You're as brave as Father was, and every bit as reckless."

Warmth filled Merrick's belly as he laughed.

Their mother turned toward them and offered a smile so bright, for a moment, all the bleakness of the world faded.

Merrick felt a strange peace now as he envisioned his father's sword hidden away in the hoard. Even though he'd lost it, he knew his father would be proud of the way he had wielded it.

Teenage Knights in Faded Blue Jeans

BRR Cannon

Another story about dragons?

I pull a handful of books off my shelf and balance them on the growing pile on my small desk.

Another story? How many times have I heard that question?

"If only you spent less time reading those useless stories, Marcus," my parents always say.

Little do they know all that reading is about to save their lives.

The stack of books wobbles, and half of them tumble to the ground. I steady the rest of the pile before glancing at the tv in the corner of my room. On the screen, cars careen into each other and through guardrails to avoid the scaled beast lumbering down the highway near my house.

This ordinary Tuesday afternoon has suddenly transformed into a story fit for my shelf. No one knows where the dragon came from, but it landed on the edge of town just in time for rush hour.

Once the ground stills, I peel my eyes from the tv and back to the mound of books. That's all of them. All of the myths, legends, and fantasy series about dragons. One of them has to have the answers for how to defeat this one.

As I pull the first book off of the stack and start to flip through it, someone pounds on the back door. Book in hand, I run through the living room and into the kitchen. Two familiar faces peer through the window.

Before I can fully open the door, my best friends bust through.

"I brought everything I could find," Liam says, dropping an armful of weapons on the kitchen table. He spreads them out for me to examine: a steel broadsword, two bowie knives, a functional replica mace, a compound bow, a crossbow, and a handful of arrows. "Think we could train the dragon?"

Kinsley frowns at the now smudged white tablecloth and holds up her contribution. "No, Liam. This doesn't look like the trainable type." She glances at me. "I just have my bow, but I have all the arrows my dad hunts with."

I nod. "Good. Now we just have to figure out which method to try and—"

The windows and walls rattle with concussive gunfire in the distance. I peer outside. Helicopters circle, but I can't see anything else.

Kinsley is the first to rush to my room, where the tv is still on. She freezes in the doorway. My heart races as Liam and I join her. A rain of bullets pours down on the dragon, but they bounce off like water droplets on an umbrella. The walls tremble as the creature roars and reaches for the nearest helicopter.

"Hurry!" Liam breaks the trance as he moves past us to the mess of books. So much for my neat collection. But this isn't the time to worry about bent pages.

Liam and Kinsley choose the first books in reach while I flip through the one in my hand. A halfling. A stolen treasure. A secret door. The story rushes through my mind as I near the end, where the dragon is defeated.

"Marcus . . ." Kinsley gasps.

I follow her gaze to the tv. Some foolhardy cameraman is tracking the dragon from the ground. Its massive claws stomp toward him in slow motion. What an idiot. He's going to get himself killed.

The dragon's scaly underbelly stretches further than I can fathom, and I realize just how big this thing is. Tall as the two-story house across the street and even longer. It's like a *kaiju* but real. How can we beat a creature like that?

Then I notice something. A dark spot on the golden ventral scales on its chest. It reminds me of something . . .

"Kinsley, your bow!"

She jumps. "What?"

"C'mon," I say. "I know what to do."

Kinsley and Liam stop their bikes behind mine. From under the trees, we watch the sight that was unfolding on tv with our own eyes. The dragon looked big on TV, but it's more terrifying in person. Smashed cars and a downed helicopter lay in its wake while another helicopter continues to circle at a distance.

"Evacuate the area," a voice blares from a police car from my neighborhood on the other side of the trees.

Everyone seems to have listened. Well, everyone but us.

My phone rings. I pull it out of my pocket. It's Mom. I answer.

"Hello—"

"Marcus," she gasps. "I'm almost home."

"Mom—"

"Just stay put, okay? Dad and Alex are at Nana's. We'll meet them there, okay?"

"But—"

"I love you."

The line goes silent. I imagine what will happen if she beats me home. She'll burst through the back door and find Liam's mace and the dirty tablecloth. She'll find the mess of my *useless* dragon books. She'll find I'm not there. If reading so much didn't get me in trouble, this sure will.

But the shaking ground brings me back to the catastrophe unfolding in front of me.

Liam thrusts the crossbow in my hands. "You sure about this?"

I muster all of my courage, just like the knights and halflings I've read about for years. "Yeah."

Kinsley hands me an arrow from her quiver. "Too bad we didn't have time to change into something more appropriate. Remember that leather armor we made in middle school?"

"Armor isn't going to help us with this thing," I say. "We're just teenage knights in faded blue jeans."

She smiles, but Liam grimaces.

"This isn't the time, guys."

He's right. We have a dragon to stop.

We wait silently under the cover of the trees as the dragon growls and trudges closer. I review the plan in my mind. We use the two bows and the crossbow to shoot at that bare spot in its scales and hope that one of us can land a shot. We use all of Kinsley's arrows if we have to. The broadsword and bowie knives are a last resort. If the arrows don't work, we go back to my house to meet my mom. But it has to work.

Finally, the dragon is within shooting distance. I can hardly breathe. Kinsley grabs my forearm and squeezes it. We nod to each other and then to Liam.

"Ready," I whisper. "Aim. Fire."

Liam shoots his compound bow first. It's close but not close enough. The arrow bounces off the scales and clatters to the ground without drawing the dragon's attention.

As Liam grabs another, Kinsley pulls the bowstring back and lets her arrow go. Her years of archery experience show. It hits the bare spot and vanishes. It takes all my restraint to keep in a whoop of victory.

The dragon rears up on its back legs and lets out a shriek that makes my blood run cold. When its feet meet the earth again, the road beneath it crumbles, and my friends and I lose our footing.

"Now it's mad!" Liam shouts.

Liam and Kinsley turn to me, like I should know what to do next. Just because I read the most doesn't mean I have all the answers. Do we run? Do we try again?

Then I realize two slit-iris eyes are glaring at us.

"Run!" I shout.

Kinsley trips on the uneven ground, dumping the arrows. Liam grabs her arm and drags her into the thin strip of woods between the neighborhood and the highway. I follow, still clinging to the crossbow and my arrow.

Before I can get more than three steps away, I'm hit with a wall of wind that throws me to the ground. I turn over and see giant wings unfurl and lift the dragon's monstrous body overhead. It scans the trees, looking for me. My friends. I can't let anything happen to them. Not after I convinced them to join me.

From here, I have a clear view of the bare spot and a chance to prove my valor. Useless? No, all that reading and imagining what it would be like to be a knight isn't going to waste now. I find every bit of courage in my veins as I lay flat on my back.

The dragon hovers directly over me. I load the arrow with trembling fingers, bring it into position against my shoulder, and aim the crossbow. I breathe in. Breathe out. Breathe in one more time. Hold it. Shove away the doubt needling my mind. Pull the trigger.

The arrow cuts through the air, and by some stroke of luck, sinks into the bare spot on the dragon's chest. Right through the wound Kinsley inflicted.

Like before, the dragon reacts. But instead of more anger, it lurches, lets out a grunt, and loses some altitude. It must have gone deeper than Kinsley's arrow or shoved hers deeper into the dragon's chest. It's a good shot, but not enough. The dragon's head darts wildly as it hunts for me.

The scattered arrows are within arm's reach. I take one, load it, and shoot again. Then again. With each direct hit, the dragon sinks lower.

Finally, it collapses on the highway twenty feet from me.

It lies still, head resting on the ground, unfocused eyes searching, chest heaving. I grab the last arrow, but I don't need to loose it. The dragon's eyes droop and close. Its warm breath vanishes in the cool breeze.

"Marcus?" Kinsley tentatively breaks the silence as she stops behind me.

Liam stands by my side. "You did it?"

I nod. "We did it."

As we wrap each other in a triumphant hug, the circling helicopter approaches and police cars emerge onto the highway from Cottage Lane. Before anything interrupts this moment with my best friends, I give them both one last, tight squeeze.

"Teenage knights in faded blue jeans," Kinsley says as we release each other. "Sounds like a new book you need on your shelf, Marcus."

Hydell's Egg

Samantha Mendell

YDELL STUMBLED DOWN the eastern trail, his eyes frantically scanning the tree trunks. "Follow the pines," he mumbled. "Follow the—"

Just ahead, the ember light of the late afternoon sun illuminated a small "20" etched into the bark of the tree. Hydell sprinted toward it, smirking as he ran. Master Yoon had been right.

"*Mark your trail on the way up,*" the dragon master had said, placing a small pocketknife in Hydell's hand. "*Then you'll need only to follow the pines home.*"

It was precisely twenty marked trees south of Gyda's Bluff, then across the Ravik River and down the forest path back to the hatchery. For once, he wouldn't return empty handed. The charcoal-gray egg, stashed carefully inside Hydell's tunic, thumped against his torso as he picked up his pace, quickly passing the numbered trees.

Fifteen to go.

Sweat streaked his brow. Hydell Jei wouldn't—*couldn't*—fail. Not this time. He'd been working for Master Yoon at the dragon hatchery for six months now and had yet to recover a single stolen egg—an embarrassment he was reminded of daily. The other dragon seekers loved to rub his nose in their recoveries. Hoisting their precious eggs high as they emerged from the Gydder Forest, they'd boast of their heroics loud enough for the sixteen-year-old apprentice to hear as he mucked the dragonettes' stalls.

But that was about to change. His recovery was going to put their measly common hillback dragon eggs to shame. His discovery would be the one to rid their land of the demonic dragons once and for all. Then the crops could once again freely sprout from the ground, no longer consumed by the demons' fire, and the skies would be cleared from the ominous Shadowland creatures.

Then his father and the other soldiers could finally return home.

Ten trees left.

A stray branch sliced his cheek, stealing his focus. Hydell's left foot hit the forest floor at an awkward angle, the momentum driving him headlong toward the towering pine. His arm shot out, just in time, and met the trunk of the ninth pine with a resounding crack.

Hydell cursed and staggered away from the tree, his vision now dotted with thick ink-black spots. Teeth digging into the side of his cheek, he stifled a scream. The taste of metal filled his mouth. His knees buckled and he collapsed onto the forest floor.

"Troll's breath," Hydell cursed again, then spat, spraying

the forest floor with blood. He tried flexing his fingers, sending a blinding pain up his arm. Instantly, his eyes filled with tears, hot and angry. It was definitely broken.

Better my arm than the—

Panicked, he reached his good arm inside his tunic. The egg was pulsing slightly; he could feel the dragonette's claws scratching against the inside of its shell.

"Thank the Keeper," Hydell said, then heaved a labored sigh of relief. The healing waters of the Ravik River could mend a fractured arm, not a shattered kingdom.

The sound of flapping wings echoed across the painted sky, the sun preparing to bow beneath the horizon. "We're so close," he whispered to the egg. "Just a little longer."

Hydell spat again and rose to his feet. Tucking his broken wrist against the egg, he began to walk, blocking the shooting pains from his mind. Heavy steps turned to a clumsy jog, his eyes fixed on the tree ahead, a burst of adrenaline spiking his nerves.

Seven. He shot past the weathered trunk. *Almost home.*

Suddenly, a distant scream of the scarlet demon bellowed across the darkening sky. She must've returned to her plundered nest.

A strange wave of pride stirred within the young seeker. Tracking a drage was no easy feat, let alone a beast of her nature. Scarlet drages were quite rare, the only breed of the mutated beasts who still possessed the ability to breathe flames after undergoing their wicked transformation. Trading their impenetrable scales for ash and smoke, the drages were hollowed shells of the magnificent dragons they'd once been, sacrificing their beauty to the Shadowlands for an empty immortality.

However, the trade was costly and left them unable to

produce offspring of their own. What they could not create, they stole. Beneath the cloak of nightfall, the demons emerged from the barren peaks of Gyda's Bluff, stealing from the dragon hatcheries of the valley. For the creatures of the Shadowlands knew that their victory could not be won if the dragons of Enger continued to rule the skies.

But, as Master Yoon often said, "Darkness always leaves its trace." The scarlet drage had stained the skies of yesterday's dawn after her late-night plunder of the hatchery's incubation hut. Her cursed fire, still simmering in her belly after claiming her prize, had produced a crimson mist from her decaying scales, leaving a blood-red brushstroke across the clouds.

Hydell had been the first to spot the mark. He'd awoken just before dawn to the cries of the dragonettes in their stalls. Racing toward the burning hut, he'd found Master Yoon instructing the elder dragons to extinguish the flames. As the flames burned to embers, the master looked at Hydell with fierce determination. He reached into his cloak, retrieving an old pocket knife, and extended it to the young apprentice.

"Follow the pines."

Master Yoon's words echoed in Hydell's thoughts as he passed the sixth-to-last tree, his fear growing. He began to sprint faster, his good arm clutching his fractured one tighter against the egg, the splintering pain dotting his vision once more. It was beginning to shake more frequently, and he almost thought he heard a tiny crack.

"Hang in there," Hydell murmured to the egg. The fifth tree was just ahead, and the path was starting to level out. Elation rose in his chest. He'd actually done it. The imagery of the other students' disgruntled faces gave Hydell a fresh burst of energy, catching a glimpse of the riverbank ahead.

"The Ravik!" Hydell whisper-shouted. "We're almost home."

But the descending red smoke put all thoughts of celebration to rest.

Hydell froze. He couldn't hear anything over the thumping of his heart. The dragonette must've felt it too because the egg began to twitch rapidly.

Snap. A tree limb crashed to the ground in front of him, blocking his path. Hydell fell onto his side, still cradling the dragon egg with his mangled arm. He shoved his fist into his mouth to keep from screaming, nausea rolled over his battered frame as his wrist knocked against a tree root.

Can't . . . stop . . .

Another branch fell, and he scrambled into the brush, crawling away from the path as best he could with his good arm. The forest filled with the sickening stench of burning ash as the maniacal cry of the drage thundered through his bones. The beast began to circle overhead, preparing to land.

Time's up.

Tears trickled down his muddy face. A whimper caught in his throat as the thick smog from the beast descended heavily upon the forest. Adrenaline depleted, Hydell felt *everything*—the stabbing pain in his wrist, the trembling dragon egg pressed against his chest.

The suffocating weight of his failure.

Hydell rested his tear-stained cheek against the ground and closed his eyes. What was Master Yoon thinking, sending him into the forest? But as his ear brushed the dirt, he heard it.

The current!

Startled, Hydell raised his head, squinting in the direction of the muffled noise. Through the scarlet fog, he could just make out the edges of the riverbank. Master Yoon's teaching rang in his weary mind. *"The fires of the Shadows cannot burn in the River."* The moment his feet touched the icy waters of the Ravik, he would be safe. And, more importantly, so would the egg.

Hydell raised to a crouched position, eyes fixed above, as a tiny spark of courage lit in his belly. A garnet shadow came back into focus, then the ugly head and ruddy form of the villainous creature, its body stretching three tree lengths long. The drage circled twice more, then dove down through the hole she'd created in the canopy, landing with an ominous thud.

Hydell's hand clutched against his mouth, silencing his shaking breaths. The creature was no more than a stone's throw away. She lowered her head and sniffed along the broken limbs. Hydell crept backward, disappearing farther into the underbrush. The drage slowly turned, her head now opposite of Hydell and the egg. Her tail swiped in a vicious circle, demolishing the underbrush where Hydell had been just moments before. He forced a small breath as the drage swiped her tail again, this time clearing three trees in the process—an opening!

Now or never.

Hydell broke into a full sprint toward the river, running parallel to the trail and passing the third, then second to last pine. His steps were noisy, loose twigs snapping underneath his ruddy boots, but it didn't matter. Silence couldn't save them now.

From behind, he heard the mighty swish of the drage's body turning once more, followed by a deafening cry. The drage breathed a thick flame across the trail, igniting the trees at Hydell's back. Ash and smog smothered the air, and Hydell's lungs clenched within his chest.

Ahead, the Ravik River flowed steadily, its silvery-blue water radiating in the glow of the drage's flames. The sound of the current drowned out by the thundering footsteps of the scarlet drage quickly closing the gap between them.

The last pine tree came and went in the blur, and Hydell almost shouted with victory when a menacing rumble tore from behind him.

Then his world erupted in scarlet.

The drage's cursed flames licked across his back, incinerating his thin tunic and searing his skin. A guttural scream exploded from his lips, and Hydell fell to his knees. The impact shook the dragon egg from his grasp, and it tumbled toward the river.

"No!" Hydell cried. With a final burst of adrenaline, he lunged forward, barreling into Ravik River—egg in hand. Waves of icy water splashed across the drage's claws, disintegrating her ashy flesh. Bellowing in agony, she took to the skies, leaving behind a wake of crimson dust.

Relief flooded Hydell's battered frame. The healing waters of Ravik gently stitched the mutilated flesh across his back, carrying Hydell downstream. A tingling sensation rippled through his wrist as the shattered bone pieced itself together. His pain was no more.

Slowly, Hydell stood to his feet and waded to the riverbank, clutching the trembling egg against his chest. The night's air nipped at his exposed back, what remained of his tunic now charred and draping awkwardly. "This was my favorite shirt," he groaned.

Hydell hurried through the forest's edge, finally reaching

the border of the Enger Valley. In the distance, he saw the glimmer of light coming from the hatchery. Master Yoon stood at the gate, a small torch in hand, the rest of the dragon keepers lined the paddock fence.

Emerging from the trees, Hydell held the egg high above his head. "For Enger!" he hollered.

The other keepers roared in applause, shouting and howling in celebration. Master Yoon's laughter rang above the boisterous noise—a sound the valley hadn't heard since the war first began.

Suddenly, the charcoal egg began to heat. Hydell quickly lowered his arm. The top of the eggshell shot in the air, lifted by an eruption of golden sparks. A tiny head poked from inside the egg, its ruby-red eyes fixated on Hydell. The dragon snorted, spraying Hydell's tunic with embers.

Hydell laughed. "You're a spitfire, all right."

The dragon squeaked, then shuddered—as though embarrassed by its first roar—as Master Yoon slowly approached. The creature eyed the light from the dragon master's lantern with cautious curiosity.

"Well done, m'boy," said Master Yoon. He placed a hand on Hydell's shoulder and gently squeezed, his wrinkled eyes brimming with tears. "The Keeper's Flame will burn once more."

The Keepers of Memory

Elizabeth D. Marie

A nantah without its rider is like a body without a soul. Where man may live on and traverse the known kingdoms by other means, we, once bound, have no recourse in our unmatched grief. As a body cannot live without a soul, so are we marked to perish with the last breath our rider breathes.

—Ren'ira

THE SHADOW OF A DRAGON circled the tall pearlescent tower, gleaming above the clouds. The two-legged beast alighted on the edge of the balcony, folded in his wings, and nosed his way between one pair of sheer midnight curtains hanging between the great marble columns.

His rider stood confidently upon the golden saddle at the base of the *nantah*'s long scaly neck, his expression grim. The rider's short, golden hair gleamed nearly as bright as his gold-trimmed armor in the blazing sun.

A dark-haired young woman balanced behind him, and through the mind-speak of his *nantah*, the rider addressed her. Because the people of Kysim—the sky kingdom—were unable to speak for themselves: *"I should not have brought you here, Solandis. This is a tomb."*

But Solandis quickly dismounted to step further into the large, columned chamber, where a beautiful sapphire *nantah* rested at its center.

"Adrastus, she still draws breath. How can it be?" Solandis whispered.

Her voice caused Ren'ira to stir. The dragon's delicate nostrils flared. She snuffed, and her hot breath stirred the curtains, their movement making the fabric shimmer like stars. Her golden eyes opened, but though her gaze shifted with the awareness of the presence of others, she did not even lift her sapphire-scaled head from the marble floor to acknowledge them.

Adrastus's *nantah* blinked and craned his neck toward the prone form. In his own voice, he mind-spoke to Ren'ira, *"Your rider has perished. Why do you not follow its soul to the afterlife?"*

Ren'ira refused to open her thoughts to him, and he arched his neck in haughty disdain at being ignored. The expression complimented the veiled abhorrence Adrastus attempted, most poorly, to conceal.

On the heels of his thoughts, the *nantah*'s voice changed

to the voice of his rider. *"Solandris, you are punishing yourself unnecessarily, and while you are yet in mourning for your husband. Let this* nantah *have her dignity in death."*

"No," Solandis's voice cracked. Her strong emotion in that simple word caused Ren'ira to curl her claws in reflex. The sapphire *nantah* heaved in a single, deep breath, while it felt as though it cost every ounce of willpower she had to do so.

"Solandis," Adrastus groaned. He dismounted. *"Her soul is empty. Look, she draws breath, yes, but see how much effort it takes. It is only a matter of time."* The rider paced to Ren'ira's side and stared at her with a critical eye. The clink of buckles accompanied the tread of his boots crossing the marble, and Ren'ira's wings shivered at the familiar sound. How she missed the feel of mounting the wind—the tang of stardust salting the clouds and soaking into her scales—when she and her rider, Elion, soared high!

"Leave me, Adrastus," Solandis declared.

The boot tread stopped. *"What?"* Adrastus spun on his heel.

"Leave me!" Her tremulous cry filled the chamber and caught in the wind, to echo into the sky dome above. The sound reverberated as it fell back down, quivering across Ren'ira's hide and resonating within her horns.

Adrastus clenched his hands into fists at his sides, a look of fury twisting his handsome features. He glared first at Solandis and then at Ren'ira. *"My brother was a fool to marry a Tirdaman,"* he spat, the venom of his hatred saturating his dragon's mind-speak. *"Someone from the earth kingdom can never understand the ways of the sky!"*

Ren'ira did not have the heart to snap her jaws or spew flames in response, though she wanted to, not appreciating how ill Adrastus would speak of her rider, who could not be here to defend himself. Instead, she snuffed again and closed her eyes against his cruel expression.

The quiet whoosh of air signaled Adrastus and his dragon's departure, but Ren'ira did not open her eyes again until, moments later, a gentle hand traced her right horn, and the scent of honeysuckle and jasmine warmed her nostrils.

Solandis gathered her skirts and knelt beside Ren'ira's head, facing her, and kept her hand against the *nantah*'s horn as she gazed into her golden eyes with tears in her own earth-hued brown ones.

This woman of the earth kingdom was not beautiful. Ren'ira had argued with Elion that she had never seen anyone plainer. Why had he not chosen one of the radiant Kysimian maidens? She had been disgusted with his choice, at first, not understanding what he could see in the strong-boned Tirdaman.

But, with time, Ren'ira had come to recognize the beauty Elion saw in her—a kind of beauty which time and age would never tarnish. Her soul was a stronghold of light that came straight from the radiant Tree of Shashar and was as deep as the life-giving waters of Nesham.

Solandis spoke now to Ren'ira, an ache in her voice, "Elion named you well, *nantah*. You are beautiful and strong. And you carry the remnants of my husband's soul inside you, as any worthy keeper of this realm. I believe there is much more to you then anyone would dare imagine."

A tear slipped down her cheek, and she pressed her hand along Ren'ira's tapered snout. She leaned closer, as if to impart a secret, and murmured, "If I can survive with only the memories, then so can you."

> THE SOULLESS NAKASH ARE AS SAVAGE SERPENTS, WITHOUT WINGS OR FIRE, YET ABLE TO SPREAD THEIR DESTRUCTION FAST AND WIDE AND TURN TO ASH ANYTHING THEY TOUCH. EVEN NOW, AWAY FROM THE BATTLEFIELD, I SMELL THE SCORCHED EARTH; EVEN NOW, I HEAR THE SCREAMS OF FELLOW SOLDIERS PERISHING IN THEIR PATH.
>
> —BERENGAR

Solandis's long, dark hair, braided at the sides, hung tangled down her back. Shadows pressed deep beneath her eyes, making her skin look bruised from lack of sleep. Ink-stained fingers moved with haste in her tasks upon the top of the gilded desk. She kept her head bent, making notations on the open parchment to her left, then turning to peruse the open book to her right, flipping pages back and forth. With her forehead pinched and brows furrowed, she wore an identical expression to Berengar while he observed her restless activity.

Berengar crossed his arms and leaned back against the open doorframe. Had he made himself presentable enough, to not add to her worry by having missed a bloodstain or a smudge of ash? He wore a fresh uniform, and his leather armor had been cleaned and oiled until it fairly shone. But it was difficult to look relaxed when his muscles were still tense from battle and his instincts still tuned to expect enemies around every corner.

This reprieve from action felt entirely unnatural, and the dragons he had encountered on his way here, soaring the sky kingdom by their great wings, with their riders, made him all the more ill at ease. Because their base brethren roamed the earth, and he should be there, fighting alongside his king to end their reign of terror.

Berengar cleared his throat, trying to come up with something clever to say to his always-cleverer sister. Solandis gasped and looked up, her quill jerking against the parchment to leave an unflattering ink splatter over the word she had just written.

She stood quickly and flew into his arms, even as he took a step forward to meet her. "You came," she whispered, voice rough with relief.

Berengar clasped his sister close and shut his eyes, absorbing the feel of her trembling form. She had always been the stronger twin, and it was hard for him to see her this way. He bowed his head, resting his forehead against her shoulder, and sighed out all the tension in his body. His eyes shut against the nightmare of battle that haunted him. "It is good to see you, Sol," he murmured gruffly. "I am sorry for the circumstances." She was far too young to be widowed, barely a year wed.

Solandis drew back and cupped his unshaven face between her hands, peering at him, reading him better than he wanted her to. "You look a mess, brother," she said softly.

"I have come from the battlefields. Our war against the soulless—" Berengar stopped himself, pressing his lips into a hard, grim line.

Worry drew her brows together. "And our king? How fares he?"

"My king gives up more and more of his soul light so that others might live," he answered, voice husky and gruff with anguish. But the tension in his jaw, and the way he spoke the words, revealed his anger. Could his sister even call the Tirdaman king hers, when she had forsaken her heritage and abandoned them for the starry world of dragons?

"You blame my husband's people for not sacrificing more," Solandis determined.

"We are dying, sister." Tears glistened in Berengar's eyes, and his own brows pulled together, creating deep grooves in his forehead. "How can you, of all people, stand by and watch us get slaughtered?" He gazed up a moment at the grandeur of the circular room in which they stood, stretching above and below them, the walls filled floor to ceiling with books and scrolls. "How can you stand here, in this place of books and parchments, so unaffected by this fight for our very existence?" He looked at her, hard, voice harsh with warning. "One day, sister, the wingless serpents will come to your door, and will you be ready to do battle against them then?"

Tears dropped, one from each eye, as Solandis stared back at him.

Berengar jerked in a ragged breath, and released it with a hiss of realization. "Forgive me," he muttered. "It is not that you have not suffered." He turned his gaze aside, and closed his hands into fists. "I came to bring you solace, not shame."

For a long moment, there was no answer. Then Solandis touched her twin's shoulder and crossed the floor back towards her desk, which sat at the end of the long, tapered balcony jutting over the abyss of bookshelves. Back to Berengar, her voice echoed in the chamber, "Do you know what this room is?"

Berengar put his head back, swallowed hard, and gazed at the dome ceiling several stories above their heads. "A scholar's paradise?" he answered sardonically, lips quirking in a forced smile.

Solandis had long ago perfected their mother's patronizing look, and seeing it now almost made Berengar chuckle. "This," she said, facing him now as she spread her arms, "is the library of memories. The sum total of all we are, ever were, and will be. We keep them and protect them, as we have been charged to do from generation to generation, since the beginning of our time."

"You?" he questioned, brow raised.

"*Us,*" she insisted. Taking a few steps his way, she explained, "You and I are a part of this charge too. Time trekkers like you gather the memories of our people first, and those memories are channeled here—carried in the soul lights —to this place, to be preserved for eternity. A task I have chosen to embrace. One day, Shashar will return and reclaim us. He will take the words written here and breathe life back into them. He will set kings in place by these words and destroy others by the same account."

Berengar shook his head.

"You are a soldier, and have been trained to survive. To only see what stands before you, face-to-face with you. But do not lose sight of the bigger picture. Of the promise that transcends the present time." Solandis continued, "Every man and beast who has ever breathed will be remembered for what he has done with the time he has been given. Think of the reward that comes after life. You cannot change what others think and believe, whether they act or do not act. You have only yourself to account for." The tears were spilling down her cheeks again, and an ache formed a lump in Berengar's throat. Where she had always been so certain of the unseen future, he continued to struggle with the concept. Solandis gazed at the books. "Elion is written here, and I will protect his memory. He was a good man, Beren, worthy of a crown not just for the way he lived his life—short as it was—but for the goodness of his heart."

Berengar's skin itched beneath his armor, and he shifted uncomfortably.

Then Solandis focused on him again, a light in her eyes. "There is someone I want you to meet."

ONCE WE LIVED FOR THOUSANDS OF YEARS, UNLIMITED IN OUR REIGN OVER THE STARS AND KINGDOMS BELOW. THEN, FROM THE HEAVENS WE FELL. WE WERE GIVEN A CHOICE AT THE TIME OF OUR FALLING, IN ORDER THAT WE MAY LEARN FROM OUR DEMISE. THAT WE MIGHT LEARN WHAT IT WAS LIKE TO WEEP.

—REN'IRA

A stranger entered her domain; she sensed his presence before she lifted and turned her head to observe him. He smelled of earth and blood and sweat, although his uniform and armor were pressed and polished.

Solandis stood beside the stranger, and spoke softly in introduction. "This is Ren'ira. She is all that I have left of Elion. I have no child to look upon, but what soul of Elion remains I see reflected in Ren'ira's eyes." Her gaze was steady and shining on the sapphire *nantah*.

Tension radiated from the stranger's stiff stance. Wariness

and mistrust. Ren'ira had never felt that before from anyone. But something more intrigued her, stirring inside her, about the man. He looked so much like Solandis, in masculine form, that she immediately knew him to be the twin brother she had spoken of before with Elion many times. Berengar. A time trekker. A soldier of the earth.

Berengar spoke, looking back into Ren'ira's steady golden gaze. "Has she forsaken her oath then? That she still breathes?"

Ren'ira snuffed indignantly, but Solandis spoke quickly. "Her survival is nothing short of a miracle, and not a sign of disloyalty. She is special, Beren. Her mourning is . . . indescribable. Yet she lives on. For what purpose, I do not know. But I refuse to let her perish, nor to be disparaged and mocked for her brave survival by riders like Adrastus."

Berengar's brows raised. "Your husband's brother. He was more against your union with Elion than I was, and willing to make a scene even at the ceremony to try and prevent it." He scowled. "It is difficult to imagine how those two could be related." He put out a hand and cautiously approached Ren'ira, taking in her appearance: her folded wings, clawed hind legs, the great horns on her head. Ren'ira was smaller than most other dragons, at only about twice the size of the *ashpar* —those mighty war horses favored by the men of the earth kingdom.

Ren'ira watched him come without outward reaction, impressed that he would brave coming closer despite his distrust of her kind. Had he ever even seen a *nantah* up close before?

Instead of touching her, Berengar stopped near her head and crouched to balance on the balls of his feet. He set his arms atop his bent knees as he studied her, but Ren'ira could not read his thoughts because only a binding could make that possible.

"I asked you here, brother, because I am afraid for her," Solandis whispered, urgency tainting her voice.

Berengar frowned, but did not take his gaze from the *nantah*. "Why is that?"

"Because if she does not die as expected, they will order her execution. It is more important to them to preserve their way and understanding instead of consider that there is a greater or nobler purpose for her survival. They do not see how remarkable she is; they only fear her. If she recovers—a healing no one would believe possible in the thousands of years since they began to serve us—the people of Kysim will turn on her. She is an abomination in their eyes."

Berengar's eyes narrowed, creases appearing in the outside corners of his eyes. "And what am I to do about it?" he asked warily, twisting his torso to look at his sister. "I am just a soldier from another kingdom; I have no standing here."

Solandis pressed her lips together, choosing her words with care. Her hands were clasped together before her, fingers knotted, as if ready to plead her case. "You are right to warn us that war is coming, even here. We do not understand the enemy we are facing. You are going to need her to survive. She will keep you safe, because my heart . . . cannot withstand another blow."

Berengar's eyes widened. He straightened, violently, and took a stumbling step back before pulling in a deep, sharp breath. His reaction caused Ren'ira to raise her head and crane her neck towards him—a motion she rarely found the will to do since Elion's death. There was an essence, warm and glowing, inside Berengar—a soul light—that only a *nantah* had the eyesight to see; a rare essence that encouraged her to respond to him. He was no dragon rider, but he had the heart of one.

But Berengar responded to the suggestion with horror, "You speak of abomination, but I am a time trekker. I am of Tirdamah, not the kingdom of the skies. And I am no dragon rider."

"It is not impossible! She needs you as much as you need her!" was Solandis's impassioned plea. "She has so much to offer you. She is wise, strong, stubborn, and cunning. You are more alike than you think!" She glanced quickly over her shoulder, into the darkened doorway which led to the spiral staircase descending down the tower—the only way into the chamber besides flying on a *nantah* to its balcony.

Then, noticing Ren'ira's reaction to her brother, Solandis gasped softly. "Look, she is responding to you!"

Berengar scowled, fisting his hands. His lips parted to answer, but a distant shout carried on the high wind interrupted his words. Solandis spun towards the tower stairs to the slap of boots ascending. Gasping, an attendant appeared in the doorway. "My lady Solandis!" he panted, his eyes wide with terror. "A creature has breeched the city. It is attacking the dragon riders—heading to the citadel!"

"What?" Solandis cried in astonishment. "How?"

The attendant only shook his head in bewilderment.

Berengar's expression darkened. He gripped the hilt of his sheathed sword. "*Nakash,*" he spat in a low, rumbling tone. "The soulless are here."

A deep horn blast reverberated through the air, and Ren'ira's wings shivered.

> I could not leave the fires of war unscathed, and I thought I understood the sacrifice I would make as a soldier for my kingdom. I am not afraid of death or the pain of many wounds. But I did not count on how indiscriminate those fires would be; how they spread and consume all within their path, even the innocents. I was not prepared to survive when they did not.
>
> —Berengar

The courtyard outside the citadel swarmed in chaos as Kysimian civilians fled for cover and dragons with their riders took to the skies. A gray haze of ash and smoke veiled the brilliance of the sky kingdom's pristine pearlescent and gold towers. Several outlying city buildings were a ruin of marble and stone that had crumbled into heaps of ashy debris. And this, Berengar knew, was just the destruction one soulless could cause.

He did what he could to help direct those fleeing near him as he ran towards the serpentine creature. But nowhere would be safe unless they could slay the beast. And if more came? He pushed away that thought to focus on the task in front of him. He held his sword at the ready, and charged.

He could not bear to look at the bodies. Already, more than a dozen lay dead in the *nakash*'s path, while the *nakash* scuttled up the side of another short tower. Its stubs where wings should have grown ended in single curved talons, which it used to climb. Where the talons punctured, marble and stone sizzled, smoked, and crumbled into ash, leaving small craters behind. It would not take much more before this tower too became a pile of rubble.

A *nantah* and its rider swooped low, too close, as the *nakash* whipped around, coiling its snake-like body, and lashed its long scaly neck to snap its fanged jaws. The *nantah* screamed as its wing tore in the serpent's mouth; the dragon struggled to correct its floundering flight, flapping its uninjured wing furiously. The dragon twisted its head around and spewed an inferno on its attacker. The *nakash* screeched more with rage than pain, but released its prey.

Another dragon swooped down to attack the *nakash*. It plucked up the *nakash* in its claws, ripping ribbons of blood across the serpent's obsidian back. The *nakash* writhed and twisted, stabbing at the *nantah* with its lethal talons, but the *nantah*'s hide protected it from any deep wounds. The scrapes those talons managed to inflict smoked only a moment, without seeming to inflame or poison the dragon.

The dragons, it seemed, were impervious to the *nakash*'s talons, just as its brethren, in turn, were resistant to the dragon fire. They were the most well-matched in a fight. The dragons may succeed at outwitting this dangerous enemy, where the frailty of man had thus far failed. So long as they kept clear of the *nakash*'s snapping, tearing jaws.

By this time, Berengar had arrived at the base of the smoking, pock-marked tower, breathless from his run, squinting through the ashy haze. The fighting reptiles screamed and screeched into the atmosphere; the sound shook him to his bones, and made the center of his gut quiver.

The shapes separated suddenly in the air, and the *nakash* plummeted, still writhing, toward Berengar. A breath later, another shadow swooped over Berengar's head, and he was plucked up by the shoulders in a *nantah*'s claws.

Berengar shouted in surprise, nearly losing his grip on his sword. But he caught sight of the sapphire dragon holding him with stunned surprise. "Ren'ira?" he shouted. A moment later she had carried him several yards and dropped him on his feet in the middle of the courtyard, to land beside him, drooping and exhausted from her flight.

"Breach!" shouted a dragon rider, swooping low overhead and calling attention to anyone who could hear. "A creature has breached the library of memories!"

"*Solandis*!" Ren'ira's mind-shout punched Berengar in the chest. "*She is in the library*!"

Of course his sister would try to protect the library of memories, even though she was no warrior, and certainly no match for the *nakash*. Berengar bolted for the citadel doors, and Ren'ira's shadow fell over him as she followed close behind. Teeth bared in determination, Berengar gripped his sword and plowed between two out-coming guards before they might consider him a threat and bar his way inside.

Though he had traveled this way only once before, only an hour ago, it was not difficult to know his way. The library tower stood at the heart of the citadel, up grand staircases and down a massive central hallway. His head and his heart pounded together in rhythm with his footfalls.

Ren'ira leapt ahead of him at the last moment to barrel through the doors first.

Berengar heard the *nakash* within screech, and then he skidded across the marble inside as well, almost losing his footing. Ash coated the floor. The domed roof was gone, debris littering the floor. Solandis's desk had been crushed beneath a large chunk. Loose parchments scattered and floated on the wind tunneling down through the opening.

And Berengar's sister lay prone beside the desk.

His heart lurched. *No!*

Bits of ash sifted down over his head. The hissing scuttle of the *nakash* as it circled the wall behind Berengar was his only warning. Berengar ducked and rolled to the side as the serpent crashed to the floor, snapping its jaws in the place he had just been standing.

Ren'ira spun and spewed flame into its face.

The soulless beast shook its head, distracted by the sapphire *nantah's* inferno. Berengar seized the moment and attacked, whipping his sword with precision towards the *nakash's* legs and tail. One slash of his sword drew a line of red between its scales near its shoulder, a second slash an even deeper wound along its torso. Berengar leapt back as its tail lashed toward him.

Then Ren'ira pounced, closing her jaws around the *nakash's* throat. The creature writhed for several moments, trying to break free. But Ren'ira clamped down harder, and the beast grew still, and then limp.

Berengar breathed hard, lifting his sword just in case. The *nakash* did not rise, even when Ren'ira crawled off its back and collapsed, eyes rolling closed in weariness. He set a hand with concern on the *nantah's* horn. Her nostrils flared. "*I will be all right,*" she reassured laboriously.

Then Berengar's eyes widened, as the rush of battle and rage retreated, and he was reminded of his purpose in coming to this room. He turned. "Sol!" he cried, rushing to her side and collapsing to his knees.

His sister, lying on her back, stared at him, breathing quick and shallow. Berengar moved to touch her face, but stopped himself at sight of the multiple burn lesions. These wounds he knew all too well, having seen them marring the bodies of fallen soldiers on the battlefield. She had not been struck by falling debris; the *nakash* had attacked her.

Horror swelled in his throat, bringing a roaring emotion and flood of tears he was ashamed to let fall, but could not stop. His breath came tighter; his lungs screamed. His heart cracked wide open.

She looked at him knowingly. "Beren," she whispered. "Do not cry."

He shook his head, denying the tears. But still they fell, coating his cheeks, his lips, burning his eyes. "No," he choked out thickly. "Do not go."

She shifted her head slightly against the floor. Her gaze went beyond him, to Ren'ira, who had lifted her head and gathered her legs beneath her again. "I will always be with you," she murmured faintly, and her hand fluttered to press against Berengar's chest, over his heart. "So long as you live, a part of me lives on . . . too." Her words faded, and her eyes lost their light.

Berengar sobbed, curling over his sister's body, until he was gasping for air and looking around in wild desperation. But there was nowhere for his grief to go; no way to express himself but to scream into the empty chamber as the emptiness inside him expanded, threatening to swallow him whole.

Then Ren'ira stepped quietly to his side, bent her long neck, and caught Berengar's gaze. He held her gaze, finding there a lifeline of understanding he would find nowhere else. "*I know what it is like,"* she said, sorrow in her eyes, *"to have your soul divided."*

She spread her wing over him like a shield, and he pulled Solandis into his arms and mourned.

Berengar did not know how long he remained. He lost all concept of time and space, and merely drifted on the currents of his unbearable sorrow. He had just laid Solandis back onto the floor when the doors banged open behind him, followed by the clack of dragon claws, then a moment later by the clink of belt buckles and heavy boots treading towards him.

Ren'ira had retreated to one side. Berengar turned to face Elion's brother, but remained kneeling before his sister.

Adrastus's armor was dulled by soot and ash, though his stance was no less regal and emanating with power and purpose. His *nantah* stood several yards behind him, waiting just inside the doors, a bloody gash running jagged through the scales of his neck. The wound appeared superficial, and the *nantah* craned his neck to take in the damage to the room before centering his gold gaze on Berengar.

Adrastus's gaze flickered Ren'ira's direction. The fear was there, just as Solandis claimed, and with a hint of loathing Berengar knew would only grow. *"We sacrificed five riders to bring the creature in the courtyard down,"* Adrastus bit out coldly, via his *nantah*, whose reptilian gaze narrowed. As if it were Berengar's fault the attack had even happened.

Glaring, Berengar lashed out, "Now you begin to scratch the surface of the losses we have suffered." He staggered to his feet. It amazed him how a broken heart affected the strength of his limbs. Each breath tore first through that broken center of his being and made speaking all the more difficult. "Even one *nantah* could give us a chance, if you had only joined my king when he called for your aid in the first place!"

Adrastus's chest expanded with fury, as his *nantah* arched his neck haughtily. The dragon rider looked down his nose at Berengar. "*Get out. There is nothing left for you here.*" With a dismissive glance at Solandis, Adrastus turned and remounted his *nantah*. They withdrew as abruptly as they had arrived.

"*You must do as he says,*" Ren'ira said in a subdued tone, bowing her head over Solandis's body. Her gold reptilian eyes stared into Berengar's red-rimmed brown ones. "*Like it or not, they will find a way to blame you for this. But there is a chance,*" and she lifted her head regally, "*that my kindred and the other riders will understand the importance of this war, and will side with your king, once the ash settles.*"

Did it even matter anymore? Berengar gazed at his sister, in a battle of despair. He swallowed with difficulty, shifting his attention back to the dragon. "My sister may have been right. You are not safe here either."

"*An abomination,*" she agreed. "*Yes, I know.*"

They looked at each other for a long moment, understanding forming between them.

"Then shall we be an abomination together?" Berengar rumbled hollowly. Solandis was right: they needed each other. Now more than ever. And besides, his king still needed him.

Ren'ira smiled with a regal tilt of her horned head. Berengar had not known a *nantah* was capable of such an expression. "*Are you ready to taste the skies, dragon rider?*" Her eyes glittered. "*You may never wish to taste the earth again.*"

Desert Cry

Rienne French

I REMEMBER THE FIRST TIME I saw the Crier.

Mumboio and I had been night fishing. We thought the beast was a man by its call, until it arched its long neck and hissed a warning at us through a slender muzzle. Pale skin resembling webbing and eyes as black as the mamba's kiss, it gazed at us from afar. The creature sat with its haunches in the waves and its teeth sunken deeply into the belly of a great shark.

Our village has stories of sea dragons from the days of the great fathers. However, these demonic beasts, with the ability to steal both the voice and life of any creature they encounter, had not been seen on these shores in a hundred years. Only the Crier's eyes followed my brother and I as we observed his feeding. Slowly, we had circled our boat as it brooded over its prey in the shallows. It was foolish to tempt the beast of legend, but the curiosity of youth had overpowered our caution.

The dragon was a big male with black spikes running down its long neck and a powerful tail. Its body was not much larger than a man, but muscular forearms gripped its prey like my older brother wrestling a boar. Long webbed claws protruded from padded feet designed to traverse both sand and waves.

Each time our vessel neared the grotesque scene, the serpent let out a deep growl that should have come from the chest of a lion. The growl crawled through my skin like maggots in a carcass. The voice did not belong to the slimy abomination from which it came but had been stolen from one of the great cats.

Memories will not change the past. They only serve to inform the future.

Now, I quickly scan the tideline. The gazelle is calling piteously from where I placed her on the sand. Not long ago, I would never have considered baiting a trap with such a creature, but much has changed. The doe writhes, broken with her back legs crushed by a rock. I didn't cause her injury, but I will exploit it for my hunt. I only hope that my prey heeds the call soon, and I can release her from the pain. I have already killed an approaching jackal. Its body lies black on the moonlit beach, but the carcass will not dissuade the creature I seek.

"Azibo, you have the patience of a barbet," Mombio said to me a fortnight ago. My eyes had forgotten the hunt and were watching a brightly colored bird flit above us.

"Your face looks like a barbet," I grumbled in response to the insult.

"Not everything is a race, little brother." He watched the herd of impala move closer to our position as I should have been doing, but I was young. "You must wait for your quarry to become comfortable in your presence before striking. Be patient."

Mumboio's chastising rings in my memory as clearly as the waves now crashing on the shore. I breathe slowly and remember everything that he taught me about patience on the hunt. I dare not move and betray my location. Cool sand itches as I lay half covered in grit. My body aches to the deepest muscle, and a fiery shooting pain runs through my buttock and down the length of my leg. Arms bent precariously with an arrow fitted to the bow string, I wait. There is no way to tell when the Crier will make his appearance tonight. I will wait as long as necessary. I will wait for Mumboio.

"You worry too much," my brother laughed four days ago when I suggested that we make the journey back to our village. I was afraid that sighting the sea dragon was a bad omen. "The beast may never frequent these waters again," Mumboio said. He thought it wise to learn more about the creature and see if it planned to reside in our winter fishing grounds, so we stayed. Camping on the beach, we watched the waves for any sign of the beast. As the days passed without another sighting, my nerves relaxed. I should have heeded my instincts.

The gazelle has quieted and lies panting vigorously. It was her voice drifting in the night air over the rhythm of the tide, not her blood, that was my lure. Now I fear my lure is forfeit. Straining my eyes to perceive any movement along the shore, I contemplate the gazelle's silence. She is useless to my cause without a voice but perhaps I don't need her voice.

Loosing my arrow to relieve the gazelle of pain, I move my mouth into the position needed to imitate its call. I roll my tongue slightly before forcing her cry from my lips, shuddering at the idea of using the Crier's hunting technique. It feels a cowardly falsehood, but Mumboio has taught me much about the need to improvise. The cry is a good likeness. Tonight, I will put all of my brother's knowledge to the test. Tonight, I will hunt for Mumboio.

The ocean devours the sand like a hungry maw until it is forced back upon itself. The repetition of the waves resembles the ragged breath of a dying animal, nagging at my thoughts. I have heard such a sound hundreds of times on the hunt, but there is no describing the moment when someone you love draws their last breath while lying in your arms.

"I thought you were taken," he had said as I cradled his broken body. It had only been the light of my torch that had forced the Crier to leave my brother in the water's shallows. Roused from sleep in the dark of night by a man's scream, Mumboio and I had split up to search the beach. I hadn't found so much as a footprint and had only stopped to rekindle my torch when the man began to scream again. Tearing through the sand towards his cries, I sprinted to the stranger's aid. As the man's screams suddenly ceased, they were echoed by Mumboio's.

Arriving at the scene within seconds, I swung my torch as a club to drive the Crier back into the waves. The dragon hovered above my brother's body. Mumboio's spear stuck fast in the sand next to the serpent. The Crier had not feared the weapon, but it did fear the light of the torch. Snapping its jaws, the beast bellowed like a hippo at the burning flame before steadily retreating to the water. As it submerged into the ocean, I ran to Mumboio. Too much damage had been done to my brother's flesh. He lay in the shallows with more blood than water lapping against his body. I realized with a sob that his life was ending and cradled his broken form to my chest.

"Azibo, I came to your screams," my brother said. Gently I stroked his brow as he coughed. It was the Crier who had called out for help. The imitated human screams were the hunter's lure, and we had been its prey.

"Be at peace, brother. I am here," I soothed, but my heart writhed in anguish. How could a warrior such as Mumboio face this end? His strength slowly slipping from him and leaving him as helpless as a babe?

The memory is too fresh to let linger. I cannot mourn Mumboio tonight. Not with what must be done. Forcefully, I loosen and tighten my grip on my brother's spear as it lays at my side. My fingers brush the slick gray skin of the mambas. Two dead snakes hang from the tip of the spear, mouths bound open, and fangs bared. I remember when my brother first taught me to beware of the mamba, whose venom could be lethally injected even after death. I will have to be close to use the weapon with the shaft broken, but this has always been my intent. I would see the whites of my enemy's eyes as the beast lies soaked in his own blood.

The gazelle's call emerges from my lips again, and this time when I call there is a splash from the nearby sea in response to the cry. I ease another arrow into place and wait. Not long after, a pair of eyes shine in the moonlight above a nearby sand dune. Too close to the ground to be a lion. Slowly, I maneuver my position towards the dunes. I had expected the Crier to come from the sea, but perhaps that was an ignorant assumption. Focusing on the spot where the eyes disappeared, I listen to the never-ending rush of the waves.

The points of light again pierce the darkness. Closer this time. They sway from side to side as the creature travels across the sand like an eel through the water. A thin muscular body is silhouetted against the sand. This is not a desert scavenger like the jackal. Its path seems to focus on the gazelle, but the beast glances at my hiding place before sliding behind a dune. My heart pounds and I ready myself. The Crier approaches.

Rising silently to my knees, I aim my bow at the place where the eyes should next appear. Too much time passes. The creature should have crested the last dune. A slight change in the wind brings the smell of rotting flesh and brine over my shoulder.

Pivoting quickly, I loose my shot with only a second to grab the broken spear shaft. I throw my body sideways. The Crier lands in the spot I vacated, his shoulder nearly pierced through by the arrow shaft. Leaping to my feet, I thrust my weapon, but the dragon dodges the blow. I am forced to give ground before his snapping fangs.

I must avoid his grasp.

Lunging again, I pierce his neck right above the shoulder with the spear tip. The fangs of the mambas stick fast in the creature's flesh. With their bodies secured to the shaft the snakes are preventing the spearhead from sliding deeper into the dragon. He snaps and claws at me just out of reach.

The Crier drives me back with another advance. We dance at two ends of a pole, neither able to strike the other until the beast twists sideways and forcibly snaps the bindings holding the snakes. They fall to the sand beneath his feet. Without the mambas acting as guard to the shaft, the dragon claws his way up the spear, pushing the blade slowly through his body.

Glancing over my shoulder, my heart sinks. I cannot let go of the spear to retrieve my bow from where it lies. Calculating the distance, I know that the beast would slay me before I could reach it. As ineffective as the spear is, it is all that is holding the Crier at bay. Taking a step backwards, I stall for time while the poison does its work. The dragon edges his way down the shaft slowly, his claws draw closer and closer. I am forced to retain my grip on the spear while the dragon shreds the flesh of my forearm.

Clenching my jaw, I embrace the pain. I will not cry out. I will not give him my voice.

The serpentine body inches up the shaft. I am forced further backward, until we fall over the body of the gazelle. The spear shaft drops, and in his blood lust the Crier seizes the gazelle.

As I scramble away from the beast, my hand falls upon the arrow still in the deer's neck. I yank it free and ready myself.

The Crier rips his fangs through the carcass. When the gazelle does not respond, he drops her body and turns his attention back to me.

Opening his mouth, the dragon produces a perfect mimicry of the gazelle's cry.

I slash at his face as he charges. The arrow lodges beneath his jaw, narrowly avoiding his fangs. The Crier vomits gore all over himself before charging again. This time he misses me completely. Blinking his eyes erratically, I notice that his jaw hangs stiff and slightly out of alignment, paralyzed. The mamba's poison has begun to take effect.

Rushing to the body of the nearby jackal, I retrieve another arrow. This time when I dodge the dragon's claws, I thrust the arrow into the gap below his eye socket. It snaps as the tip lodges in bone. The beast slams his paralyzed muzzle into my chest, hurling me to the sand, but I have caught a glimpse of Mumboio's spear beneath the body of the gazelle.

Two steps and I reach the gazelle. The Crier is right behind me, his breath labored.

I pivot the spear like a club. Catching the creature in the skull, it knocks the dragon to the sand. Lying beneath my blade the beast screams for help with my brother's voice.

Infuriated by this, I drive the spear into the dragon's heart, silencing him forever.

It is finished.

Every inch of my body throbs with adrenaline and pain. My forearm is bleeding badly from the dragon's claws but the wounds are not deep.

Mumboio is avenged. Blood has been repaid with blood and life with life.

The Crier lies dead in the sand pinned by the spear of his last victim. I fight the pain in my arm as my abdomen tightens and a new agony blossoms within me. Grief. I will return to the village with the head of the serpent as an offering to our mother. My brother's life will never be forgotten, but with the death of the sea dragon, I hope to one day forget the circumstances of his death. It was Mumboio, his wisdom, his instruction, that killed the Crier, not I.

Mumboio will have the credit for the dragon's death, and his name will be known as the greatest hunter this land has ever born.

Dawn of the Dragon-Son

H. L. Davis

THE RAIN ON THE ROOF isn't the only pounding to be heard within the isolated forest cabin.

Rap, rap, rap.

At the table, Rayner stills, his heart hammering in his chest. He slowly draws a sleeve across his upper lip to wipe away some grease from his evening meal. His other arm lowers to his side, fingertips brushing the hilt of his knife.

Rap, rap, rap! "Is anyone home?" A muffled voice seeps through the cracks around the door. "I'm lost. I need shelter."

A child? Rayner creeps to the door, pausing a moment before lifting the latch. This could be stupid. But what if someone truly does need help? Running a hand through his wild black hair, Rayner takes a deep breath and opens the door a couple of inches.

A thin line of lantern light illuminates the gloom to reveal the figure of a boy not many years younger than he. He is swallowed in a cloak far too large for him, a hood concealing most of his features except for a timid smile. "Beg your pardon, sir. I've never been in these woods before. May I stay here until this rain slows?"

Rayner scans the darkness behind the child. He doesn't sense any other presence in the shadows. His lips a firm line, he nods and opens the door wide enough for the unexpected visitor to slide through.

Once inside, the lad throws off his dripping cloak and hurries over to the fire. He takes a long, hard sniff of the rabbit stew. "Smells good! Can I have some?"

Rayner shrugs, finds another bowl and spoon, and ladles out a helping. Grabbing it, the boy takes a seat at the hearth. He shovels a big bite into his mouth—then lets it fall right back into the bowl. "Smells better than it tastes." He sticks out his tongue, setting the food beside him.

A strange sensation tickles Rayner's throat. A chuckle? But he rolls his eyes and sits at the table to resume his own meal.

"I certainly hope this visit ends more pleasantly than it's begun"—the boy's voice deepens drastically—"Rayner Azar."

Rayner leaps to his feet, drawing his weapon and spinning around. "Seer Larkin!" His eyes shrink to slits as he looks at the old man now sitting before the fire. "Really? Taking the form of a child to gain entrance?"

"Desperate times call for desperate measures." The seer lifts his gaze to Rayner, cerulean eyes bright against his dark, aged face.

"I've seen your soul's embers glowing from afar many months now, faint but alive. And I've tried to give you solitude. Time to grieve. But the enemy is coming, Dragon-Son. They've learned of this island and plan to take control. The people need you."

"They need *me?*" Rayner stares. "Surely I'm the last dragon you'd come to for help."

Seer Larkin's frown deepens. "Indeed, I fear you may well *be* the last dragon."

His dagger clatters to the floor, and Rayner's mouth grows dry. "So it's true, then. All the others. They . . ."

"Surely you didn't think they'd go these three years without coming to find you?"

"It would serve me right!" The words fly like arrows. "If only I hadn't fled that day on the mainland. Maybe I could have . . . could have . . ." A sound, half sob, half growl, escapes Rayner's throat. "But I'm a coward. I saw their cannons. Their nets. And I—"

"You were afraid." Seer Larkin rises to his feet and takes a step toward him. "I won't praise what you did that day. But I do understand it. You were thirteen, and your first battle was one of the fiercest I've ever seen. With new weapons to bring down even the dragons." The seer rests a hand on Rayner's shoulder. "But perhaps the Maker had his own reasons for you to run. Perhaps he knew your greatest battle was still ahead. A time when we would most need you to be brave."

Rayner shoves the man's knobby fingers away, his amber eyes blazing. "I'm no hero. Go, old man. Before I make you leave."

With a ragged sigh, the seer walks across the room. "Our spies say the enemy sails for the western shore even now. They'll be here at dawn. I implore you, Rayner, to reconsider. Fight for the people. For those you've lost." He dons his cloak. "And fight to forgive yourself." Seer Larkin slips through the door and melts into the night.

Rayner grits his teeth, hot tears flooding his vision. Kicking his chair over with an unbridled shriek, he sinks to the floor, the deluge outside powerless to drown his wails.

The clouds weep a steady drizzle as Seer Larkin gazes across the waves Seven large shapes show stark against the pale horizon. Rows of men wait along the shore—most, armed with swords; a lucky few, with shields. They stand hushed in the chill of the salty sea air as their doom draws steadily closer.

"Is there no chance, Seer? Any way we can at least protect the women and children?"

The old man turns to face the whispering fighter beside him. "I used the last of my power to speak with Rayner Azar. All that's left now is to find our courage and hold fast."

The blood-red flag of the enemy flickers from the mast of each approaching ship. Seer Larkin closes his eyes to block out the sight when an unmistakable sound shocks them back open.

The roar of a dragon.

From the cliffs behind the small army, a black beast leaps into the air, smoke pouring from his nostrils as he soars over the water. Panicked voices shout in the distance, and Seer Larkin raises his fists. "Fly, Rayner! Fly!"

The men on the beach yell and clang their weapons as the dragon nears the boats. Unblinking, the seer watches, hope fluttering in his chest like a sail in the wind. But a fresh cheer is smothered in his throat when a net shoots from the foremost vessel, speeding toward the Dragon-Son.

A monstrous maw of cords opens wide to swallow him whole. Rayner wobbles in flight, snarling as he swerves to avoid the trap.

The net plummets empty into the sea.

Rayner dives toward the attacking ship, the skin between his dark scales burning red as he closes in on his target. Splashes sound as enemy soldiers jump from the boat, desperate to escape the coming wrath. Rayner opens his jaws, eyes bright, armored body flashing as he sets the towering masts ablaze. He sweeps to the next vessel, and the next, until four of the seven ships are engulfed in flames.

Pumping his wings, Rayner rises skyward and scans the final three ships. Another net is being made ready to bring him down. Teeth bared, he dives like a thunderbolt toward the cannon, knocking it to the deck with a resounding clang.

Rayner circles the remaining boats, his skin glowing scarlet once more as the fire within him swells. His throat tightens as he remembers his fallen dragon kin, as he hears the voices of the people they swore to protect carried faintly on the breeze. With a burst of light, Raynor roars, fury and valor flaming from his throat to devour the last-standing ships.

Black smoke billows to the sky. Ebony wings spread wide, the dragon returns to shore. Amidst cries of awe and victory, Seer

Larkin elbows his way through the crowd to reach Rayner Azar. Breaking through the throng, he finds a flickering mist enveloping the dragon's large frame. It dissipates to reveal Rayner back in human form, gasping for air, hands on his knees. Seer Larkin stares open-mouthed at the boy.

Rayner meets his gaze with a wobbly grin. "Well, old man. How did I do?"

The seer's eyes shine. "Dragon-Son . . . I do believe your best is yet to come."

SAMSON TENEBRIS
AND THE
VIAL OF SOULS

HOLLY MALEY

NOW THAT I SEE HIM, I do want to kill him.

But I have not walked into the dragon den to destroy, but to trade. Father sent me on a "critical mission" —my first one, actually, and he prepared me for this specific task and nothing more. My woolen tunic and breeches look anything but dragon-proof, but they are woven with protective runes of my father's own design. That is to say, they are enchanted by the most powerful sorcerer since Merlin (if you believe Father's tales, which I *sometimes* do).

Despite this, I find myself acutely aware of just how small and insignificant I am compared to the beast before me. I stand in a great cavern under a mountain, illumined by the gentle light of the pinecone-sized orb floating at my side. Its orange glow glimmers off innumerable coins, gems, jewelry, and other precious items that form a small hill in front of me. Lying on top of it, the dragon. Snesiphus the Destroyer.

I can't help but be awed by the sheer size of him. I have faced many strange and dangerous creatures in my sixteen years as part of my father's rigorous self-defense training: three-headed dogs, eagles made of lightning, and other beasts that plague the nightmares of man and child alike. None of them compare to what lounges before me.

The dragon's head alone is the size of a cart horse and his scales are so black that in the dim light Snesiphus seems more like a void than a living being. But the worst thing about him is his eyes—red and blazing with almost palpable malice. They are the eyes of one who has burned entire villages to the ground just for pleasure. I have seen some of his ruins, I know just how much this creature deserves to die. But enchanted though my sword may be, it is no match for dragon scales. No blade is.

I pull out a gold crown from my satchel and hold it out to him, despite every instinct telling me to run, stab the dragon, or do anything but play nice.

"Where did you find such a thing?" Snesiphus asks, his voice a landslide. I can hear the greed in it—the tension he struggles to contain in his words—and see vindictive desire swirl in his oversized eyes. The crown is expertly and intricately crafted, a prize by anyone's standards. But it is also an ancient relic of the northern peoples, worn by none other than King Giles the Magnificent, who legendarily tricked a dragon into servitude some centuries ago. If that dragon was Snesiphus himself, I cannot wager a guess, but to all dragons the name

Giles is anathema.

Snesiphus tries to be subtle, to disguise just how much he craves the crown in my hand, but subtlety does not come naturally to one who levels villages with a single breath. His head leans in and his claws inch forward. I can sense rather than see his every muscle strain as he refrains from seizing the prize for himself.

"Information is not free, Destroyer, nor is it part of the deal," I say. "I'm here for the Vial of Souls. Give it to me and the helm is yours. Take it for yourself, and you'll find it's imbued with a powerful curse that only I can remove."

"Yes, I can smell it, boy. You need not explain dark magic to one who was forged in it."

The dragon looks at me with timeless eyes that know no haste. It's hard to breathe in the stifling air. I itch to be anywhere else, but I know better than to rush him. At long last the dragon sweeps his long tail across the horde and slides its tip through the handle of a dark crystal vial, just one more bauble in a sea of priceless knicknacks. He dangles it in front of me. "I accept," he says, but moves the vial away when I reach for it. "*If you answer one question.*"

I grit my teeth. "What's your question?"

"Why does your father seek a soul extractor?"

So that's what the vial is. "I don't know. He doesn't tell me ev—" I start, realizing my mistake. I never mentioned my father. In fact, Father specifically instructed me *not* to mention him. Before I was born, he usurped Snesiphus from his domain, exiling him to the east. Only recently, while my father has been occupied with other matters, had the dragon returned. But dragons do not forgive.

"I could smell Tenebris on you a mile off, boy. Now answer the question."

I resist the urge to squirm under Snesiphus' gaze. Father never did tell me the function of the vial, and now I can see why he evaded the subject. I have always known Father to be a hard man with a past, but a soul extractor seems dark even by his standards—not to mention unnecessary. He already has a thousand different ways to destroy an enemy that don't require rare and specialized relics.

But I have to answer the dragon, so I say, "To remove someone's soul."

"But whose soul? And why?"

"That's three questions. The deal was for one."

Snesiphus' mouth twists into what I think is a smile, exposing yellow and black teeth, each longer than my hand. "You know how to play the game, boy. Good. You will need that wit to survive the coming days. I will ignore your insolence this time because I look forward to your reaction when you do find out what Tenebris has planned." He slips the vial next to my feet and I pick it up. The vial is empty and unnaturally cold, as though it strains to suck away all warmth and life and the only thing preventing it is the little silver stopper on top. I tuck it away in my satchel, careful not to jostle the stopper loose. "Now the helm."

I place the crown on the mound of coins. Father said that if I willingly passed it on, the curse would be lifted. Nothing feels different, but Snesiphus seems satisfied—or at least he doesn't try to stop me when I back out of the cavern towards the exit tunnel, my glow orb following close at my side.

Just when I'm almost out of his sight, his rumbling voice

calls out, "Young Tenebris." I tense, worried the curse hasn't been lifted, or that the dragon has changed his mind and is about to swallow me whole, runes or no runes. "A word of advice: to destroy a dark lord, ask yourself where his heart lies."

I'm sure he means my father, who still insists on calling himself *The* Dark Lord, despite having done nothing of any real diabolical significance in my memory. Fatherhood tamed him, some say; he became paralyzed by paranoia for his only son's safety, and obsessed with his research. He has been looking for something my entire life, as if his own life depended on it. This Vial of Souls is the key to whatever consumes him. Why else would he risk sending me off?

Now Snesiphus is suggesting that I might destroy my own father, the man who had defended me my entire life. Does he think Father is plotting against me?

That he would use the Vial of Souls on his own son?

My stomach crawls as though filled with scarabs as I follow the tunnel to its exit high on a mountainside. I breathe the crisp air deeply, willing it to clear my thoughts. The legends warn about how dragons worm into your head. I should have taken them more seriously. Now I can't shake the idea that Father has been protecting me for some purpose that has nothing to do with love.

I berate myself for even thinking such things. Whatever else he is, my father is first and foremost my *father*. I may not know all his intentions, but I do know those of Snesiphus. Beasts like that exist only to corrupt and destroy. As I descend the mountain, my insecurities about my father morph into hatred for Snesiphus. I hate him for his mind games. I hate him for his pointless greed, for his callous destruction of human life.

And most of all I hate him for making me feel so powerless. I have trained as a fighter my entire life only to be made completely helpless when faced with real evil.

Remnants of men braver or more foolish than I litter the mountainside: bones, shields, swords, and arrows, blackened and broken. I wonder if these reckless souls would do it all over again if given the chance. Was it worth dying for something that would never be? Their deaths, however valiant, failed to defend anything.

From this elevation, all I can see is miles and miles of devastation. At one time, this may have been a beautiful view, with sloping green hills covered in spring flowers leading to a lush forest. But now the mountain is completely barren save for only the most stubborn of weeds creeping through the rocks. Black scorch marks streak the forest farther out and I'm surprised Snesiphus hasn't burned the whole thing down, such is hatred for living and wholesome things. But then I realize that the streaks form a pattern. From this height, it looks like an eastern glyph. I am not well versed in the eastern tongues, but the character is familiar enough that I am able to piece together its parts to decipher its meaning.

It's the glyph for "destroyer." The dragon marked the land with his own moniker, much like I used to scratch "Sam" on the underside of wooden tables as a child. Except this was no wooden table, but the very land people depend on. The last stroke of the character passes straight through a village, now empty and charred.

This is all a game to him.

As the only son of a retired dark lord, I am not unaccustomed to the company of questionable characters. I have supped with those who would sell their only child for wealth, stab a brother to save their own skin, or lie through their teeth to win a woman's heart. But at least with those people, there was some semblance of purpose. I could understand the *why*. But there is no *why* to justify this level of wanton destruction. Suddenly I understand how these men whose bones lie scattered before me could throw their lives away so recklessly. They understood better than I that real evil does exist, and they aimed to exterminate it or die trying.

Something in me snaps and the voice of practicality vanishes. I have no idea what I am going to do, what I *can* do, but I refuse to do nothing. I turn around and ascend the mountain once more, careful not to disturb the relics of those who once attempted and failed at what I'm about to attempt. They lead me right into the mouth of the tunnel. Before I have time to think, I unsheath my blade and bellow, "Snesiphus!"

My voice echoes off the cave walls and amplifies to something powerful, almost fearsome. For a moment I am strong, righteous, and ready, my blood boiling and my sword glinting in the orange light of the orb which has never left my side. My heart is a war drum spurring my feet onwards, straight into Snesiphus' treasury.

Both the dragon and the Helm of Giles remain exactly where I'd left them. The dragon, lying on his horde; the helm, already forgotten amid the excess.

"And what do you intend to accomplish with that sewing needle?" Snesiphus says, eyeing my sword.

"Plunge it into your heart and rid this land of your poison!" I say with more confidence than I feel. Seeing the monster once again in his fullness cools my blood, but I already challenged a dragon. My death sentence is as good as signed. The only path is forward.

Snesiphus lets out a low grunt—a chuckle, I think—that rattles the gold coins under him. He rises to his feet stiffly, as though he has not bothered to move for hours or even days, and steps down from his self-made hill to tower over me. On his feet, he scarcely fits in the cavern. His head scrapes stalactites off the ceiling as he maneuvers it to face me. The sulfur churning in Snesiphus' belly burns my nostrils, his breath an acrid wind against my face as he sneers, "Go ahead then."

He moves his head aside to expose his chest, taunting me closer. I am absolutely certain it is a trick—only dragon teeth and claws can pierce dragonhide—but I have no better ideas. At least by playing along I might delay the inevitable.

My heart pounds and the hilt of my sword slickens as I break into a cold sweat, but I edge forwards, forcing myself to control my breathing and thus also control my nerves. Breathe in. Hold. Breathe out. Pause. Again. Step after step.

I walk so close to the dragon that I can feel the warmth from his body and see a faint, rhythmic vibration just above his left front leg, slow yet steady. His heart. Snesisiphus watches intently as I plant my feet in the ground, grip my sword with both hands, and thrust it upwards with all the strength I can summon.

The steel sparks and bounces off the scales without so much as scratching them. The strike does more damage to me than to its target, rattling my entire body and dislocating my right shoulder. Apparently Father's runes don't protect from self-injury. Only now do I realize that a small, irrational part of me really did believe that I could at least damage the dragon.

That hope now crumbled, all that's left is a stone in my stomach, a stabbing pain in my shoulder, and a single thought: *I'm going to die.*

The dragon laughs so deep the very stone under my leather soles trembles. That laugh seizes me with cold terror. I can hardly think. Snesiphus growls, "My turn," and opens his mouth wide enough to swallow me whole. Only when his stained teeth are mere feet from my face do my battle instincts take over. I dive to the ground and somersault, my satchel slipping off my shoulder in the process. The dragon's jaws clamp down where I was a split second earlier, narrowly missing my glow orb and sole source of light. The orb darts to my side as Snesiphus follows up by sweeping a massive claw at me. I reflexively sidestep and parry with my offhand, and with that single, familiar action something shifts in me. I remember who I am. I am a warrior, son of *The* Dark Lord Dominus Tenebris, and I have trained my whole life for a moment like this. I will not be devoured by evil without a fight.

Dragon claws carve deep gashes into the stone behind me and the force of the blow knocks my sword out of my hand. Before I can grab it, Snesiphus whips a spiked tail my way and I duck behind a large boulder to avoid it. The top of the boulder shatters as the tail strikes it and huge chunks of rock rain over me painlessly, repelled by Father's enchantments. That makes for three successful defenses against one of the most fearsome beasts known to man. *Hope* may be a strong word for what I feel; perhaps *strength* would be more fitting. I will likely die in this cavern, but it will not be as a coward.

Snesiphus' raw power is constrained by the walls of the cavern and cannot match my speed. I feel alive. Battle sings in my blood, focusing all my senses on a singular goal: survival. This saves me for a short time. I focus on dodging, but the dragon's rising fury is destroying the cavern—and my cover— bit by bit. Too many blows and Father's enchantments will wear off, and I'm so focused on defense I can hardly spare a thought for offense. What could I do? Go for the eyes? I have no sword. Hold out until Snesiphus collapses the cavern on us both? I am not sure that would even vex the ancient beast while I would not be so lucky.

My stamina flags, but every foiled attack only increases the dragon's ferocity. Eventually he loses patience entirely. "Let us see how you dodge dragon fire, little cockroach," he says after I barely skirt another tail swipe. His black belly begins to glow red. I snatch the glow orb to my chest, flatten myself behind the gold mound, pull my hood over my head, and pray the runes on my clothing hold.

Snesiphus lets loose an inferno that cracks and rages around me. Sweat pours from my face as the flames rage hotter and hotter, burning the very air until I can no longer breathe. All I am is frenzied need: need for air, need for the cool touch of water, need for it to *end*. When the onslaught of dragon fire finally vanishes, I am left slick with sweat, gasping and coughing on the cave floor, desperately trying to catch my breath in the smoky haze. The air I do gulp down smells of soot and tastes like bitter metal—or is that the stress from my own strained body that I taste?

I cannot say how long it takes for the air to clear enough for my cough to subside. It takes a few more breaths until my head also clears. I do not realize how tightly I grip my glow orb until I free it from my stiff, aching fingers and let it float above and beside me. My shoulders tense at what the light reveals: the runes on my garments have faded away. They did what they could and now I am left alone, defenseless, and almost too exhausted to care.

The gold horde before me fared far worse. The top layer of coins oozes over mangled artifacts from untold ages; the Helm of Giles itself lies half-molten, sinking into the treasures beneath it. I dimly wonder if King Giles will welcome me in the afterlife, if he will be impressed by how long I lasted or disappointed that I failed and ruined his helm in the process.

Snesiphus regards all this with eyes wider than I thought possible. His head sways to and fro as he takes in the wreckage, then rises upward to let loose a terrible roar. The cavern shakes. Chunks of rock fall from the ceiling, tearing at my less-than-magical garments and into my skin. Then his gaze finds me: small, broken, coated in soot, yet slowly rising to my feet despite his best efforts. Fire and ice war within me: I am a fearsome warrior fighting against impossible odds while also a little boy cowering after a bad dream, blood cold and palms clammy.

"Look what you've done!" Snesiphus snarls.

What use Snesiphus could possibly have for such riches, I will never know. He has no love for beauty, no need for trade, and yet he paws at his horde desperately, a bereaved creature at his beloved's ravaged side. I would almost feel sorry for him if only he had lost something worth weeping about. As is, the sight is pathetic, but it gives me an idea. An idea and a desperate, very ill-considered plan.

In his distress, the dragon is momentarily distracted. I *could* use this as an opportunity to escape. If I was wiser, perhaps I would. Instead I crouch low and run as quickly and quietly as I can around the gold pile, using it and then the stalagmites as cover as I make my way to Snesiphus. Or more accurately, to my satchel, which lies closer than I'd like to the mourning dragon. I find I'm holding my breath and I force myself back into a familiar breathing pattern to still my racing heart. Breathe in. Hold. Breathe out. Pause. With no weapons or armor, stealth comes naturally, and the dragon is so devastated he does not notice me slip the satchel on my shoulder even though I stand no more than ten paces away. I creep away and begin unhooking the latches on my pack.

I'm halfway back to where I started and unreasonably hopeful that this might be as easy as it seems when the dragon's head whips my way. He growls low and flings out a fanged tail. It smashes into my stomach and swats me aside like a ragdoll, spilling the contents of my satchel onto the cave floor before me. The spikes miss my vitals but slash my left thigh. Running is no longer an option, but I thank whatever gods are watching over me that Snesiphus actually knocked me closer to my target.

I roll onto my good leg, snatch the Vial of Souls from the ground and crawl towards the treasure. I'm still winded from the tail strike and every part of me aches, but I press forward, the rough ground scraping into my knees. I try not to focus on the pain, the enraged beast, or fruitless thoughts of the afterlife, and instead fixate on the cold glass vial in my hand. I swear that it calls me. It craves to be used, to consume whatever life it can find.

Almost there, I tell it silently, dragging myself within a few feet of the dragon's stash. By the time Snesiphus repositions his bulk for another attack, I'm where I need to be.

As soon as Sensiphus sees the vial, he knows what I'm

doing. I can see it in his eyes: the slow, bewildered fear of one who is not used to fearing.

I don't allow him time to process this unfamiliar emotion. Instead I give the vial what it wants, opening it and pointing it directly at the treasure: Snesiphus' life's work, his obsession, the thing he values above all else. Some might say it *is* his life, his very soul. It's a huge gamble on my part, but desperate times make all men gamblers, and in this case I seem to have guessed correctly. The vial warms and glows in my hand as something like red flame slithers off the gold and swirls into the container. Snesiphus' soul. His greed had been so ancient and so fierce that his very life became bound to a pile of useless trinkets.

I can hardly believe it's working, that I am actually besting a dragon. I can't help but taunt: "Go for the heart, you said?"

I immediately regret it. Snesiphus' face contorts as his belly begins to burn anew. He will risk dragon fire once more, risk the further destruction of his precious treasures, if it means stopping me.

The last tendrils of red spiral from the gold and into the vial. I flick the stopper back on, trapping the soul of Snesiphus the Destroyer inside. And yet across the cavern, the dragon still stands. Evidently it is not enough to merely trap the soul; I'll have to destroy it too. But how? If I smash the vial, will the soul be set loose once more?

Snesiphus gives me no time to think. Flames begin to spout from his mouth. On instinct alone, I roll to the side, all pain forgotten, allowing the vial to clink to the ground where I had just been. I keep rolling as far from the flames as I can, the mound of gold once more positioned between me and the dragon. I hear the roaring flames before I see them; they claw over the gold above my head, singeing my hair and scorching my clothes. Seconds longer and I would have been engulfed, but the flames are short lived, replaced by a screech of pain so high and piercing I worry it will deafen me even through my hands pressed against my skull.

Then silence. Perhaps I *am* deaf, for no dragon could be that quiet, least of all one so maddened.

Unless he is no longer living.

I rise to my one good knee. My blistered and bleeding body protests as I peer over the gold pile, careful not to touch the scalding metal. The vial has vanished entirely, obliterated by the dragon's own breath. Snesiphus himself lies dark and motionless on the cave floor with his head embedded in molten gold that encrusts his right eye.

Something brews within me. The desire to laugh, dance to unheard music, and shout to the heavens. But it is tempered by disbelief. I half expect to wake from a bad dream, or for Snesiphus to rise from the dirt and finish the job. I stumble to my good foot and limp to his corpse, needing to touch it to believe it. I run my hand over scales smooth as glass with edges sharp as knives, warm to the touch yet rapidly cooling. "Thanks for the advice," I murmur. He does not stir, and for the first time since I challenged the dragon, I begin to breathe easily. My shoulders relax and a smile takes over my face. Subdued at first, but then wild as the reality sinks in. I laugh. The sound is foreign in this bleak, deathly cavern, but I can't hold it in, and soon uncontrollable laughter echoes all around me as though the great heroes of old laugh with me, witnesses to my triumph.

I came as a simple errand boy, I would leave as a dragon slayer. I'm not sure how to wrap my mind around that, but one thing I do know and it cuts my laughter short: Father will be furious. Not only did I risk my life needlessly and against his explicit directions, but in the process I lost the artifact he searched for for as long as I can remember.

Yet I can't help but wonder if that's for the best. The dragon is dead, but his words live on. Intuition tells me Snesiphus was at least partially honest, that Father's plans with the vial are not wholesome. Regardless of whether they endanger me specifically, I may be the only person who can do something about them.

I would sooner face another dragon. Not because Father is more terrifying than Snesiphus, but because he is not. It may just be easier to face pure evil than your own flesh and blood. I'm not sure yet how I will confront Father, but I know it will not be with a blade.

Nor will it be by hiding.

THE WOODCARVER'S PUPPET

KAYLA E. GREEN

I PULLED THE FINE-BRISTLED BRUSH across the smooth wooden surface, leaving a trail of glittering gold in its wake. Admiring the outlining of the scales of the dragon marionette, I leaned back in my chair. The project was finally complete.

Pride ballooned in my chest only partially distracting me from my stiff upper body and the fact I felt more like 60 than 16 sometimes. My neck ached from the afternoon's work but hunching over a table with concentrated efforts for long periods was worth it when looking at what I made with my hands. Woodworking was a family artform and I was proud to have learned the trade from my uncle.

I smiled to myself, thinking Uncle Gepetto would be so

excited the puppets were ready to share with the children in town. No, Uncle Gepetto would *have* been excited. I physically winced at the internal reminder that he was gone, the sharp edge of grief deflating me.

I stood and walked across the dirt floor to the small window to my right. I felt the weight of the frown on my face as I looked at Uncle Gepetto, frozen in time, under the dimming light of dusk. No longer flesh and blood but cold, hard stone.

My fingernails dug painful crescents into my palms, despite my callouses, as I looked at what was once my beloved uncle. I heard my jaw *pop* as my molars clenched together. "Curse the stone plague and Gideon the Wicked!" The words burst from my mouth even with no listening ears around me.

A hurricane funneled within me, winds of anger, loneliness, and bitterness swirled with the rains of regret and desperation. Figuratively and literally, the ensuing storm threatened to cause torrential damage. Overwrought with emotions meant a purge of hurt—which had resulted in destroyed projects, torn clothes, even broken bones from hitting solid stone walls.

Stone. Tempest turmoil swirled in my chest. Even if Uncle Gepetto was gone, a part of him stood right there. So close to me. To our life together. He was the last family I had, and the stone plague took him from me.

Statues of those that once lived were common throughout the kingdom of Ranier. Gideon, once the king's most trusted knight, betrayed him and attacked the castle. And not just by sword. With dark, evil powers, and a terrible force that struck victims with a painful illness. Fever wracked the poor souls' bodies for three days, causing their minds to become hazy.

When the transformation to rock was nearing, without fail, the curse would give an unshakeable urge to move, to go outdoors under the veil of night. Within minutes of breathing the open air, stone encompassed them wholly.

No one could stop him, the corrupt knight, who rightfully earned the moniker Gideon the Wicked. There were whispers that there was but one hope to push back his darkness—the tears of a dragon. The lore said that dragon tears could cure those cursed before they turned to stone, even negating every shadow of evil with the pure love within their teardrops.

I didn't know of any dragon sightings in over two thousand years.

"Just because dragons haven't been seen, doesn't mean they aren't there. Watching. Waiting to return when people most need them." Uncle Gepetto's strong, steady voice echoed in my memory, his never-wavering hope more palpable than the belief in dragons unseen.

"A wooden marionette wearing a pink tulle dress walked through painted mountains.

"The princess wandered from mountain to mountain, urged on by the need to save her people. She neared one cave and her chest warmed. Called forth by some force greater than herself, she entered. A small light guided her through the darkness, leading her to a hatchling. A baby dragon who she named Figaro. Together, they would extinguish the shadows of evil."

I shook my uncle's narration away. On a whim, I grabbed the dragon puppet and walked outside, the night air cool but not cold. Stars littered the sky that just tucked the sun in for bed.

I stood in front of the solid stone statue of my uncle as my pulse beat loudly behind my eardrums. *What was I doing?* I swallowed, my mouth suddenly dry. Licking my lips, I spoke, silencing the tranquility of the night. "Uncle Gepetto, it's me, Jimeny. I wanted you to know that the puppets are finished." My face felt hot. With swift fingers, I worked the strings of the dragon puppet. It flew gracefully in the air, but my heart was weighted down.

As quickly as the sadness rose within me, a tidal wave of fury rushed forth.

"You had to go visit that boy whose mother had the stone plague, didn't you?" The words were bitter on my tongue as I shouted them at his unhearing ears. "Even though no one knows how it spreads on its own? Seven . . . It only took me seven days. One week to finish the dragon. But you aren't here to see it. Our imagined design made tangible." My voice caught in my throat. "*My* design."

"Gideon the Wicked deserves this fate, not you!" The world went red and a feral shriek filled my ears. I threw the puppet to the ground with a resounding *crack*. Only then did I realize my eyes had closed and the scream was me.

"No, oh no!" A sob escaped me as I looked at the shattered marionette at Uncle Gepetto's feet. The puppet was a pile of broken wood. I wrenched my hands wildly through my shaggy hair, damp from my own sweat. I pushed my palms into my temples, and fell to the ground. I pulled my back up to the stone and leaned against what was my uncle's legs.

The world around me blurred from the mist in my eyes. I rested my head back and looked up at the stars. I absently singled one bright shimmer with my gaze. "I wish there was a way to bring my uncle back."

Feeling as shattered at the pile of green and gold wood on

the grass, I had no energy to resist sleep. Slumber soon offered a welcome reprieve.

I scratched at my nose but the tickle persisted. Groaning, I leaned forward, rolled my shoulders, and cracked my neck.

I opened my eyes and blinked again and again, trying to make sense of the scene before me. A woman with blonde hair and a dress of shimmering, blue stardust smiled brightly.

"Jimeny, please don't be frightened. I am the Blue Fairy and you made a wish on my star tonight. And when you wish upon my star, no matter who you are, your wish is to come true."

The howling winds inside me dulled to a gentle breeze. "Am I still dreaming?" I pinched the skin on the back of my hand—the pricking pain sent a bolt of gleeful energy throughout my veins. I scrambled to my feet. "You're going to bring my uncle back to life?"

The Blue Fairy's smile waned, and her blue eyes softened. "My powers are limited and there is only one source of light magic strong enough to achieve such a thing."

"Dragon tears."

"Yes, that's right." She waved a hand toward the broken puppet, still lying on the ground. "Dragons left your world long ago, but because of you, Jimeny, a dragon will return." She gently waved her hand. The glittering cloud that surrounded her grew. It encompassed the shattered toy. In a swirl of blue light, the marionette was repaired. I covered my eyes against the bright flash of light. When I opened them once again, a dragon, the size of a horse with an elongated head like a camel, stood.

Tentatively, I reached a hand out. The dragon, gold trimming each green scale, sniffed me and dipped his head, almost as if to grant me permission to touch him. When my fingers touched his surprisingly smooth skin, a painless sensation of pins and needles surged up my arm.

"You and the dragon are bonded. He is your wish granted, after all," the Blue Fairy said. "Dragon tears are the key to saving those who have fallen victim to the stone plague, but . . ."

"When will Figaro's tears come?" I looked in the dragon's golden orbs, his irises seemingly glowing like fire.

"Figaro?" the fairy questioned.

"It was the name of the dragon in . . . m–my uncle's story." My words caught in my throat.

She offered a small nod and soft smile. "A dragon will only share that part of himself in an act pure of heart. But harvesting the dragon's magic to prevent further injury from the stone plague is not your primary concern. You must stop the darkness at its source or wickedness will counter with great force."

If I had been the dragon, I would have roared. My anger ran so hot in my blood at the thought of the evil behind the stone plague. "Gideon will pay for what he has done."

"I have faith you will avenge those that have been wronged," the Blue Fairy said, gracefully rising up until her feet no longer touched the ground. "The dragon knows you are his master, but take heed, dear Jimeny. Darkness in your heart will not drive out the darkness around you. Only light can do that."

I looked at the Blue Fairy hovering in the air, then turned my attention back to the green and gold dragon. "What darkness is in my heart?" There was no response, but when I shifted my gaze, the fairy was nowhere to be seen. Irritation flushed my skin at her implication.

I stroked the dragon's muzzle gently. He exhaled heavily,

his breath warm and smokey on my face. "I've always wondered what it would be like to fly."

As if understanding my words, the dragon knelt. His belly flush with the earth. My heart quickened as I threw a leg over his sleek back, feeling thankful for my tall height. And feeling ready to avenge Uncle Gepetto and all of Ranier wronged by Gideon the Wicked. Refreshed anger welled within me, Figaro huffed, and the pins and needles went up my arms.

Don't be reckless, a small voice said. My conscience? Figaro? I shook my head. It was time for vengeance.

I kicked my heels into the dragon's side, expecting to soar into the sky. The dragon huffed, a small plume of smoke exiting both nostrils, and took two steps forward. He bent his neck and sniffed at the grass.

"Figaro?" I pressed my heels into him again and patted his long, slender neck. "We need to go."

He shook his head as if saying no. Tingling goosebumps covered my arms. A tug to rethink going straight into Gideon's domain. I jerked my head back. Gideon did not deserve one more moment of peace. I had been without peace for too long.

"Fly!" I kicked as hard as I could with the back of my feet.

The dragon bolted forward and up. I gasped, feeling my body sliding. I wrapped my arms tightly around him, eyes closed tight. My heart pounded against my ribcage as if meaning to escape.

The wind slapped my face, the cool night air refreshing to my anxious bones. My pulse returned to normal and I dared to look. "It's like a painting," I whispered. The stars shimmered as if wanting to be plucked from the field of night, and wispy clouds separated us and the harvest season of the heavens with the world below full of dark and wicked things.

My jaw made an audible tick as I clenched my teeth. "Lower, Figaro. I need to make sure we are heading for the castle."

Grunting, Figaro responded to my words, drifting smoothly down below the clouds.

"There!" I leaned forward, my hold loosening around the beast, as the gray flames of the usurper of the rightful king flashed around the stone perimeter. A known trait of his villainy.

As one would direct a steed, I urged the dragon forward. Rage coursed through my veins, a need for revenge controlling each inhale of my lungs. "We're going to kill Gideon. We'll attack the guards and keep going until everything is ash! I'll . . ."

Figaro stopped mid-descent, throwing my body off-kilter. I gasped. I locked my hands around his neck again and righted myself. "What's wrong with you? I could have fallen."

The dragon growled, a low, rumbling sound. My arms flushed with a tickling chill. An internal voice whispering, *danger*.

"You're here for one reason—to help me stop Gideon the Wicked and his cursed stone plague."

Figaro turned his head at an odd angle, his golden flame of an iris peering into my own brown eyes. There were no words spoken but an odd sensation pricked my mind. I felt the dragon's concerns, questions as if they were my own.

"I know it's only you and me, no others to help fight, but you're a *dragon*. The creature of lore and legend. A beast of pure, light magic. The only plan we need is you and your fire!" I shook my head at myself, trying to reason with an animal.

The dragon whined, a forlorn, gravely sound that was higher pitched than his growl.

"There's no way we can lose. Please." My voice cracked. I watched, unblinking as the dragon seemingly nodded his head. Roaring, a nearly deafening rumble, he dived down.

Shouts erupted around the castle's watch towers and upper level as the dragon let loose a cannon blast of fire. His white inferno hungrily devoured the enemy's gray flames.

Arrows whizzed by, audibly slicing the air. Something whispered to turn back, but I ignored the voice. "Get to the center of the castle. We'll smoke Gideon out and put an end to his evil rule!"

The dragon put his ears back as he rushed onward. He jolted back suddenly. I screamed, nearly losing my hold. A terrible screech tore from the dragon's chest, and he turned.

No, no, no! "Why are you retreating? You stupid dragon. We were so close!" I berated the creature as he clumsily maneuvered the sky, ignoring the annoying tug that something was wrong. Ignoring the prickles running through my arms. "You're heading back home. I can't get revenge if we go home!"

I screamed and scolded until my throat burned. Tears stung my eyes. "Gideon knows there's a dragon. We lost the element of surprise."

Figaro let out a shriek. Clumsily, he darted forward, faster than he flew to the castle. His torso rose up and down violently with each breath. Rushing wind filled my ears and anger filled me, pushing back the whisper of warning in my chest. *Hurt.* I refused to listen.

Thud. The dragon plummeted to earth, and I tumbled off him headfirst. My back slammed into something rock hard.

Groaning, I looked to see the statue that was once Uncle Gepetto.

Something wet ran down my cheek. I *didn't* cry. Yet, tears fell. Because of the dragon running away and ruining everything. "You!"

I scrambled to my feet. Figaro was licking his leg, blood-stained from an open wound on his calf. He had told me through our bond he was hurt. I should have listened.

The dragon snapped his jowls at me when I rushed to him. I stepped back, finding his eyes. Guilt and shame flooded me, dousing every ember of wrath within.

"I told you we couldn't lose. I lied without meaning to." I ran my fingers through my sweaty, greasy hair. "Let me help . . ."

The dragon snapped again, his throaty growl following. Keeping one golden eye pinned on me, he licked his wounded leg.

Squinting, I saw something protruding from it. Bone? No, it was an arrow. The dragon had been shot because of me following my emotions with no rational thought, no plan. If he hadn't retreated, we both would have been killed. And Gideon hadn't even shown himself. The realization was sobering.

I ran into the cottage beside the workshop building. Grabbing a bucket, I went to the well and pumped fresh water. After dropping it beside the dragon, I went back and grabbed everything that was curing in the humble kitchen—three links of sausage. I also snagged a loaf of bread and a basket of figs, the only things out on the counter.

I made meager steps toward the dragon until he snarled. I took one step back and sat. If the dragon were to stretch his neck, I would be within arm's reach of him. I extended a sausage link to him. "Words can't undo the hurt I caused. But I hope, even if you don't forgive me, you'll let me help you."

The animal turned, his yellow eyebrows drooped, giving him a melancholy appearance. He sniffed and gently took the meat. Pulling it away from me, he gobbled up the whole of the sausage. I offered him the second and then the third. He took each and ate in turn before lapping water from the bucket.

He exhaled and laid his head down, dirt rising in bursts with each heavy breath.

"I'm going to get the arrow out and clean your wound." Tentatively, I walked to his injured hind leg. He watched my every move. I gripped the piercing wood and the dragon wailed. Biting back my own scream, I pulled the object free. I tore my shirt off to press against the leg, trying to stop the bleeding.

After several minutes, the shirt looked as if it had always been red. I tore my pant leg and created a tourniquet, the dragon whining softly. My adrenaline was long gone, but I pushed myself to run back to the cottage. I grabbed linens, fresh clothes for myself, and another bucket of water.

Back beside the dragon, I dipped a towel in the clean water. Blood washed away with each gentle stroke. The injury started to clot, slowly but surely. I wished my own internal wound would start to scab. To seal shut. No, I deserved the painful shame bubbling in the pit of my stomach. The acidic chagrin of guilt gnawing away at my heart to remind me that my actions were wrong.

Once more, I went to my kitchen. I rummaged until I found some herbs my uncle had gotten from the healer. I mixed them with water creating a paste and returned to the dragon.

His breathing was less intense than before and he did not

react to the poultice I packed in his wound.

The sun was shining bright, its warmth unwanted as I worked. Sweat pulled in the small of my back. Beads hung loosely on my brow. When there was nothing left for me to do for the dragon, my stomach rumbled. I grabbed the forgotten bread and basket of figs off the ground and sat leaning against the dragon's torso. I heard him sniff the air.

Gingerly, he lifted his head and neck. Figaro's eyes peered into mine as he brought his nose to my hands.

"Do you want a fig? It's my favorite."

His ears flicked and he lapped the small fruit up with his tongue. His eyes brightened and he nudged my shoulder, causing me to laugh. "You like the figs, huh? Makes sense. Your name is *Fig*aro."

He snorted. I took a bite of the sweet fruit, and gave him one. We did this until my stomach was full and the basket was empty. Absently, I rubbed Figaro's scaly back. "I should have listened to you, Figaro, and waited to go after Gideon. I need to gather everyone who is able to fight to stand with us."

Figaro's golden eyes met mine. The strange pricking in my mind gave me assurance that this was the right course of action. "Gideon won't sit idly in his castle long. I need to act before he moves tonight." I stood but hesitated. "Will you be okay while I'm gone?"

He prodded me softly with his warm nose, his scent of ash and amber warming me as well as my heart.

"You want us to believe you have a *dragon*, Jimeny?" a man, Jeffers, cried out. A handful of others in the crowd gathered in the town square laughed. "Being alone has gone to your head."

"Jimeny is telling the truth!" another voice argued. "I saw the dragon in the sky last night. Came from the outskirts of town, where the boy lives."

"Don't feed into the poor boy's delusions," a woman's voice scolded.

Anger pounded in my veins, but I gritted my teeth and pushed it down—I didn't want anger to lead to any more unnecessary hurt. "Figrao, the dragon, is real. He's injured, but he's going to help us stand against Gideon the Wicked but we *can't* do it alone."

"You can't do it at all," sneered Jeffers. "Because there's no *dragon*. And there's *nothing* that can win against Gideon. You've seen firsthand his power." He shook his head while turning to walk away. "Grow up."

"Please," I begged. Soft tickles danced on the skin of my arms. "He's almost here."

Murmurs exploded through the crowd. "There!" the man who defended me earlier yelled. "There's the dragon."

"Figaro!" I watched as the dragon limped forward, slowly emerging from the treeline. "Do you all believe me *now*?"

Everyone stared at the green dragon, dumbfounded.

"Gideon knows the dragon is here," I continued. "He won't wait long to come after him, after *all* of us. If you can wield a weapon, then fight with us for the statues who cannot, and to ensure no more fall victim to Gideon's stone plague and dark powers!"

"I will fight with you," said Jeffers, his eyes never

leaving Figaro.

"And I!" Echoing voices sounded around us.

"Men, get your weapons. Women, take the children and seek shelter." I met Figaro's golden gaze and something told me the enemy was near. "War will be here soon."

Through many people's efforts, men from the closest towns this side of the kingdom of Ranier stood with me and Figaro, ready to fight Gideon. But fighting the bitter resentment that fueled my emotional tempest, left more room for worry. I couldn't help but wonder, what if more than a leg was wounded this time? Goosebumps rose on my arms, under my sleeves. I exhaled and could see my breath. Gray lights shone eerily in the distance.

"It's time. Get ready!" I tapped between Figaro's shoulder blades and he lifted into the darkening sky. "You take the lead, Figaro," I said into his ear.

A blood-curdling cackle echoed through the night. "So, the flames were indeed from the beast of legend," bellowed a deep bravado. Gideon, wearing armor as black as the surrounding night, stood alone. No soldiers. No support. Gray flames, one on each shoulder, cast his bearded face in grisly shadows. His black eyes were sunken and black veins pulsated under his skin. He didn't look human. "A dragon will be a nice addition to my stone garden," he said. Then, snarling, he shot forth flames from his gloved hands, turning the closest man to stone.

Screams of fury and fear rose up. Some men scurried to

retreat while others rushed forward. *Flash, Flash. Flash*. Again and again, Gideon turned men mid-step into solid stone.

I stared, lost for words at the sight. I knew Gideon caused the plague, but seeing the people solidify instantly soured my stomach.

Figaro flew high and then dove, down, down. My teeth rattled with each breath I took. My knuckles were white from my grip as the wind whistled in my ears. Bright white light and heat blazed ahead as Figaro breathed fire.

Gideon yelled curses, one of his gray flames was out and a hand injured.

"Yes! Keep going, Figaro," I encouraged, leaning my head closer to his right ear. My chest inflated with things I had long forgotten. Trust. Amity. Hope. More gray flames shot toward Figaro, but the dragon darted.

In my brief reverie, I lost my hold. I hit the ground hard, all breath knocked from my lungs. Several ribs cracked as Gideon's ironclad foot stepped down on my chest. His sinister and otherworldly face hovered over me, spittle flying from his thin, cracked lips as he let out an animalistic, guttural cry.

"Watch, boy, with your last moments as I destroy the dragon and all that dared to defy me!"

I tried to scream, but my lungs felt like they had collapsed with Gideon's weight. My arms felt so weak, I couldn't even lift them. Sharp pain radiated down my back, making me feel that my vertebrae would soon fracture. My vision was spotted. All I could think about was that I didn't get a chance to properly say I'm sorry to Figaro. I didn't get a chance to make up for my wrong actions that hurt him.

Life was leaving me. I strained to catch the golden iris of

the dragon, of *my* dragon, to will him to flee for safety. To tell him to find a new master that could lead him to victory against this evil. Green and gold entered my line of sight. Gray flames struck Figaro's leg—the fire that turned victims to stone. A horrible shriek left the dragon.

"No, don't!" The words were forced and quiet, my chest straining. I punched Gideon's boot, knuckles bleeding with each blow. Blows that did nothing to push the monster away.

Ominous laughter thundered. "I have to give you credit, boy, I've not had this much fun in some time. Your death won't be quick. You and your dragon have whet my appetite for more. I think it's time to spread my flames beyond this mountain kingdom, don't you?"

Quiet whines from Figaro's throat bubbled up in the near distance. A tear ran down my face. I *didn't* cry. But for Figaro, I would cry unashamedly. Not only had I failed my uncle and the people of Ranier, I had failed my dragon.

"The dragon is trying to fight the darkness, how sweet. But futile. I'll be sure to tell the world that dragon tears and victory against me is only the dream foolish children have." Gideon's palm glowed eerily with his cursed fire.

"It's not . . ."

Gideon moved his foot. I gasped, the air filling my lungs, pushing against the shattered ribs painful. "What was that? You want to look at your dragon as you both succumb to the stone curse?" He grabbed my shirt collar and pulled me up at an awkward angle. My feet scurried to find the ground.

"Figaro," I croaked. My dragon's scales were dusted with gray from his foot up to his belly. "Get out of here! Use your tears to save yourself. Leave me! I deserve . . ."

Bright white heat surged from Figaro's snout. The ground rumbled. I fell forward and Gideon stumbled back.

Adrenaline hot in my veins, I pushed myself up. Smoke and sizzling steam filled my line of sight as dark gray and white flames pushed against each other. My eyes widened as the darkness gained the upper hand, nearly consuming Figaro's light.

I pounded my feet in the dirt. "Gideon! Let him go." Sweat dripped down every inch of me as I got closer to Figaro's side.

Gray smoke swirled as fire licked behind my knee. I screamed, a sweltering heat stinging my leg. My calf was hard, heavy. It dragged me down. White fire cauterized the dark burn, stopping the stone in its path.

Figaro roared. He stepped forward, slowly but surely. His white fire consumed everything Gideon sent his way. The wicked one's eyes flashed wide, the fear giving him a brief appearance of almost human. He grit his teeth and the black veins bulged.

In a cacophony of growling screams, Figaro's light consumed Gideon. From toe to head, in a moment, Gideon the Wicked faded to gray ash.

My head fell back to the ground. More tears fell. *Was it raining?* I wondered, so many droplets on my face felt like too much for my own tears. I fought to open my eyelids. Blinking, golden irises looked into my own. "Figaro," I murmured. "Y . . . you did it."

Figaro slowly nuzzled against my forehead. Large, dragon tears fell everywhere. With all the strength I had left, I touched his warm snout. I touched my forehead to his. *Please know, I* thought, *that I wish I had treated you better. I'm so sorry, Figaro.*

Pins and needles pricked my hands and arms. *Forgiven.* The word swept over me like a tidal wave. Finding strength in my dragon, I strained to see through the clearing smoke from my vantage point lying on the earth. A familiar form was moving toward Figaro and me.

"Jeffers," I called to the man roughly fifty feet away. "We need a cup, a bowl, something to catch Figaro's tears."

The man returned in a few minutes. Figaro's eyes closed. Tears continued to leak between his green lids. A large glass mason jar was filled to the brim with the plague's cure.

"Figaro?" I asked, but his eyes never opened.

He inhaled shakily. *Love. Always.*

"F—Figaro!" I sputtered. The looming form next to me grew smaller, smaller. Until my dragon was nothing more than a shattered marionette puppet.

I pulled myself to what was left of Figaro, not immediately recognizing that my leg was no longer heavy and my injuries were no longer painful. I gathered the puppet in my arms.

"Jimeny." Jeffers' voice was uncharacteristically soft. He held the jar of tears in his hand. "We're going to start distributing the cure. Are you going to be all right until your uncle is back?"

I swiped at my face with my shoulder, refusing to let go of what was left of my dragon. "I didn't know giving his tears meant he'd d-die."

Jeffers cleared his throat. "The legends say a dragon can only cry once. To shed its tears is to sacrifice its very magic, its soul."

I looked up into the sky, listening as Jeffers' footsteps became distant."Please," I managed through sobs, "Blue Fairy, bring him back. Bring him back, *please.*"

No fairy appeared. No unspoken wish granted. Silently, I made my way home with my dragon, my friend, only splintered wood in my arms. Home where my uncle was a stone.

My mind replayed the last word I felt from Figaro. *Forgiven.*

Figaro, you forgave me when I didn't deserve it.

I inhaled sharply as a small group stood in the yard where Uncle Gepetto was frozen. The pale blue of dawn peeked over the horizon ahead. One lone star shone in the sky. I pulled my marionette close to my chest. "I'll live to be worthy of that forgiveness," I whispered. "Always."

WINGS

MARY E. DIPPLE

MOST OF THE TIME, Abe could ignore the pain in his back. It was easier if he focused on his feet and the road before him rather than the phantom sensation of what used to be.

One day at a time.

One step at a time.

One breath at a time.

That's what the doctors had told him anyway. But some days were harder than others.

Today was a hard day.

Abe needed a distraction, and his friend Susan always had something fascinating brewing in her shop of wonders. He'd never met a human with a mind like hers. He could hardly keep up with her, and for a dragon that was saying something. Though, he supposed it was more the route she took to get to her conclusions that made his mind spin. Once he knew where her thoughts were going, he could follow the trail.

The bell on the door chimed as Abe stepped into the shop. The front room was always tidy, only a few of her more common inventions sat out on the floor. Abe made his way to the door that led to the back of the shop where the magic happened. He spied her mass of brown curls through the crack in the curtain as she bent over a large canvas, a sewing needle in hand. A smile touched his lips to see the grease smudged across her temple from where she'd obviously brushed her unruly curls away.

When she didn't turn, Abe glided up to her, his hands clasped behind his back for balance as he leaned over her shoulder. "What are you working on today?"

Her scream filled the room as she leapt to her feet, a left cross flying for his face.

Instinct alone saved Abe from a black eye as he dodged the blow and fell backward. His balance had never been the same, not since . . . Well, it wasn't the same.

Sue gasped when she saw him on the floor. "Abe, are you all right?"

Abe stood and brushed the dust from his slacks. "Yeah, I guess I should know better by now."

Sue grinned, revealing white teeth that weren't quite straight. "I was hoping you'd stop by today. I've got something to show you."

Abe returned her grin—who wouldn't in the face of her excitement? She took his hand and pulled him through the chaos of sawdust, canvas, leather, and gears that were scattered about her shop. She let go of his hand just long enough to gather up a set of poles and cloth, not unlike what she'd been working on, and shoved them into his arms.

The next thing he knew, she was pulling him out the back door and down the lane toward the town's high bluffs. Abe's heart died a little with each step as he realized where they were headed. His steps slowed as if each movement filled them with lead. This was the last place he wanted to be, today of all days. But Sue's grip on his hand tightened as she dragged him to the top of the bluff.

She grinned and turned to the vibrant green fields stretching before them. The great river in the distance looked little more than a stream. Wind scampered about the bluff and tickled Abe's hair, inviting him to play. Abe closed his eyes as moisture filled them.

"Here, give me that," Susan took the bundle of poles and canvas, oblivious to the agony constricting his heart. "I'll only be a moment."

Abe concentrated on his breathing and turned his back to the cliff's edge. It was fine. It would be fine. There was no other choice. He had to be fine.

"There."

He turned back wanting to see the smile he heard in Sue's voice. He needed that smile. What he found, though, were two triangles of canvas stretched over the poles and sitting like two large kites with a cross bar extending below each. Abe blinked, not understanding.

Sue rolled her eyes at him. "You dragons are supposed to be so smart. I swear you must have been sick when they were passing out imaginations."

Abe shook his head, a pit filling his stomach as he stared at the canvas and poles. "Sue, I doubt there is a man or dragon in this world that fully understands how your mind works. But I enjoy trying. Explain to me what we're supposed to do with these."

Her smile was like dawn breaking across the horizon at five thousand feet. "We're going to fly."

A knife in the chest would have been less painful. "Sue, I can't fly. You know that. Don't do this to me. Not today."

Sue put her hands on her hips, leaving a grease smudge on her brown trousers. She looked up at the sky. "I don't know. Looks like the perfect day to me. Come on."

She bent down and wove herself into one contraption, her hands gripping the cross bar. She squared herself to the cliff and set her face into the adorable little scowl of concentration that he loved.

It wasn't until she started running that he realized her intentions. "Wait!" He held up his hand and stepped in her path, bringing her up short of the cliff. "Does this even work? Have you tested it? I can't catch you if you fall."

Sue stood straight and let the peak of the triangle rest on the ground. "Of course I did. Two weeks ago. It's been raining so much, this is the first chance I've had to show you. Come on, lizard brain. Let's fly."

Abe swallowed hard and looked over his shoulder at the long drop. Heights had never bothered him, not until the day he'd lost his wings.

"Suit yourself." Sue shrugged and used his moment of hesitation to slip past him. She jumped from the cliff and his heart flew into his throat as she fell. After a brief moment, her contraption caught the wind and glided out over the valley.

Abe's jaw dropped in wonder as she caught an updraft and turned to fly back to the cliff's edge. "Come on, lizard brain, are you going to let a little human have all the fun?"

Abe looked from her to the remaining contraption, and a warm flutter tickled his belly. He shifted his form, skin turning to scales and bones becoming hollow. The enveloping robes that would have been his wings didn't come, just the scale armor that would protect him if he fell. A pang of grief came with the transformation and the absence of what should have been there, but the flutter in his stomach pushed it away.

It took him a moment to figure out the straps and get secured. Once ready, he stood on the cliff's edge, his eyes closed, listening to the wind as it played up and around the bluffs. When it felt right, he allowed himself to tip out over the edge and into the embrace of an old friend. The canvas snapped as the wind caught it and lifted him up.

Abe laughed as Sue let loose a cry of pure joy and together, for the first time in over a year, they flew into the clear blue skies.

The Hatchling
and the Rogue

Anne J. Hill

THE GOBLINS HAD A PRIZE my elvish tribe had spent centuries searching for: a dragon hatchling. I'd decided the day we'd learned of his location, I'd give my life to bring him to my people.

I crouched behind a tree and peeked around it. The forest stopped just short of the gully, and a rotting bridge with patches of reinforcing lumber was the only clear way across the ravine to the goblin fort. A waterfall rushed nearby, masking my sounds. From this angle, none of the goblin swine could see me, but I had a clear shot of them. After my military division had spent a few days scouting the fort, I memorized their routine. Or, what semblance of a routine they had. Goblins were not overly known for order, but that didn't mean they were immune to personal ticks and repetition.

A stout, portly guard walked back and forth in front of the fort gate, which was a mesh of sticks and mud. He was bald except for an unruly tuft of hair on his scabby head. He looked short enough to grab by the legs and toss into the ravine without much trouble, if he didn't weigh so much. Sunlight bounced off a jagged sword tied unsheathed on his hip. He took twenty steps, stopped, spit, watched it fall down the gully, smirked, and turned around to repeat the same thing on the other side. He was stupidly amused by his own antics, and his smirk never dwindled, no matter how many times he'd done it this morning. Only a goblin could be so mindlessly entertained, the uncivilized creatures that they were.

"Oi! Crat!" a voice shrieked from the gully. "Watch it, you three-teethed mongrel!"

Crat did indeed only have three teeth. I could see that much from here. "Move outta the way, skin and bone!" Crat yelled the term of un-endearment for his brother-in-arms as he spit again for good measure.

A bird call, two tweets and a short twitter, sounded from the west. That'd be Khili'thion, our ranger, and leader of our military division.

My stomach twisted in a mix of excitement and nerves. This wasn't my first mission, but failure would not only affect our tribe, but all elvish Dragon Riders to come. Being the youngest in our division at the age of seventeen, I'd worked long and hard to earn this spot. I'd prove to Khili that he'd made the right choice in selecting me from the rogue's guild. Not that he *had* much of a choice, since I was the only available rogue left who hadn't already been recruited by the military.

And once I'd proved myself to Khili, I would be welcomed into the brotherhood. I would finally *know* things that no amount of snooping had gotten me so far.

I waited several beats before whistling back a deep wallop topped with a long shrill note.

It was time.

I waved my hand over my face and shadows engulfed me, magic that made me harder to see. I rolled to the balls of my feet. It was my job to slip past the gate undetected while the others distracted the goblins. Being the only rogue in our division, I had the highest chance of making it through unnoticed. I knew magic I'd learned from the guild I grew up in and was sworn to keep it secret from all others.

I crept closer to the goblin fort, tree to tree, hiding in their blind spots I'd memorized. When I reached my side of the crude bridge, one of Khili's arrows with blue fletching whizzed through the air and embedded in Crat's protruding belly. He teetered on the edge of the bridge and splattered into the gully.

A volley of arrows rained down on the fort from the west. With everyone distracted, I danced through the shadows like a ghost and passed through the gate, fashioned out of wood, mud, and stones. Once inside, I got the first glimpse of what lay beyond the fortified wall, which had been only guesswork before.

I hid under a rickety lookout tower—a poor excuse for a structure. A mere boulder could take it down. These goblins were lucky we didn't have any giants on our side. Obscured by my magic and the little protection the tower provided, I scanned the courtyard. Goblins clogged every corner and were thickest by the great door that barricaded me from the heart of the fort.

The hair on my arms raised. I could *feel* that the hatchling was on the other side of that door. I couldn't explain how it worked, but I knew the bond between elves and dragons from centuries ago was the reason.

The goblins wanted to raise the dragon to be a fountain of magic to drink from until he was nothing but a withered corpse. They'd kill his soul and then use his magic to obliterate all of us. We couldn't let that happen. *I* couldn't let that happen. The elves had holy plans for the hatchling. We would tame him, learn to ride him, and use him to find the other remaining dragons, once again bringing Dragon Riders back to our lands. Everyone knew a dragon without a rider was a witless, dangerous beast. They needed us to flourish, just as much as we needed them.

A magical ball of fire flew over the wall and landed amid the goblin horde. I closed my eyes to avoid being blinded and bent my knees, ready for impact. The ground trembled and pitched underneath my feet. Despite my best efforts, my body flew against the wall behind me. My head throbbed and my back screamed in pain, all the air knocked out of my lungs. I cradled my head while my vision swam—not a good way to start my mission. I looked at my feet; they were far too visible. My magic puttered out when I'd hit the wall. Once my vision stopped swimming, I flicked my hand in front of my face and was cloaked before anyone noticed me.

The putrid stench of rotten eggs wafted from the spewed goblin guts. I gagged and pushed to my wobbly feet. As much as I hated goblins, the scene before me was still devastating. Goblins lay dead, some blasted to smithereens and others wailing in sorrow or roaring in rage.

This was my chance to reach the door.

I had no illusions that the door would be unlocked, but if I hurried, I could pick it open. I dodged my way through the cesspool of grief and rage. Finally at the door, I sheathed my dry dagger and worked on the lock. My hands trembled more than I would have liked. Grunts sounded behind me. I glanced over my shoulder, but no one was paying attention to me.

For now.

Shouts filled the fort as my division swept in. No time to focus on that, though. I had to think of the dragon. The sounds of battle drowned out as I focused on the lock, carefully lining the pick at just the right angle. It snagged and slipped out of place. "Come on," I muttered to the stubborn lock.

I imagined the hatchling's face when he'd see his rescuer. I would be his hero and gain the respect of my people. I would be *wanted*. All dragons had an innate trust in elves. My people and the dragons had been bonded centuries ago. Even a hatchling would feel it in his veins. The hair on my arms raised again and excitement surged through me. Closer. I was getting closer to the hatching and obtaining everything I'd ever wanted.

I worked the pick like a bard plucks his lute, and finally, the lock clicked open. I sighed in relief, glad I hadn't become goblin food.

Thud. A gnarled arrow embedded in the wooden door right beside my head. I jumped and swore. But before I *did* become goblin food, I pushed the door open, slid inside the stone fortress, and shut it behind me. The pounding of arrows hitting the door and the rampage outside faded from my thoughts. I looked up at the greater threat, and my stomach dropped into my toes.

A troll towered over me holding a spiked club. He stood

between me and the dragon's rusted cage. Slime dripped down his black teeth and plopped on the ground. He was massive, twice my height, and four goblins wide.

The room was made of stone—finally something worthy to be called a fortress—with rocky rubble scattered about the room. It stank of urine and moldy food.

The troll grunted and looked down at me with dull eyes. "Goblin?" His brows furrowed as he leaned forward and sized me up. "No. Baby elf." He straightened with a rumbling laughter. "I eat elf now."

Stupid troll. I was anything but a *baby* elf, and he'd remember that for however long he lived. His meaty hand rushed toward me. I rolled out of the way, but not before slicing my dagger through the thick skin on his palm.

He clutched his hand to his chest and roared. "Feisty food!" The troll swung his club, and the spike dug into the stone ground where I had been standing. As large as he was, he was no match for my speed. "Stupid elf," he grumbled.

I pulled out my throwing knives. The only way I could bring down something this large was to aim for his head, which was far beyond my reach.

The troll spotted me behind him and lumbered my way. With the skill of someone who'd been training since six, I flicked one knife, then the second, and they seamlessly found their marks. The troll roared and clawed at his eyes, dropping his club. That would have to do for now.

I turned to the cage on the other side of the room. The hatchling cowered inside, no bigger than a medium-sized dog.

"*Stay away!*" a voice intruded my thoughts. The hatchling backed up to the far corner of his cage with his tail tucked under him, and his wings hiding all but his eyes. His scales were blue and his flesh was littered in scars. A chain secured his throat to the rocky ground.

I held my hands up. "I'm not here to hurt you." I took a tentative step closer to the cage.

He hissed and a smoky ash puffed into the air.

I stopped. "Okay, okay. I'm Ezerth. What's your name?"

His eyes narrowed. *"Not for you to know. Elves evil. Elves chain, hurt dragons."*

I shook my head. The poor hatchling must have been confused with all the chaos. But couldn't he feel how safe I was due to our bond? "No, the *goblins* hurt and chained you. I'm here to free you."

"Take me home?"

My attention was drawn back to the troll as he stumbled, his hands blindly searching for me. He swung and the tips of his sharp fingers nearly grazed my cheek. I jerked back, found a rock, and tossed it to the other side of the room. He barreled after it, slammed into the wall, and thudded on the ground. He twitched, groaned, and stilled. As far as I could tell, he was dead or knocked unconscious.

I looked back at the dragon. My talking had alerted the troll to where I was. *Can you hear my thoughts?*

"Yes. Hear all elves' thoughts. Bonded, bloodied."

What did that mean? *Well, I'm here to take you home, yes. Can you promise to not burn me if I open your cage?*

He stretched out his small wings and stood. He had to crouch his head low to keep it from banging against the spikes on the top of the cage. *"Elves not trusted. Ezerth takes me to his home, not mine. Cages. Whips."* He clawed at the rock ground.

"Zakŏr wants to be free."

Is that your name? Zakŏr? My people have no intentions of chaining and hurting you.

Zakŏr hissed again and I got the impression that he hadn't intended on revealing his name. *"Yes. Elves capture dragons. Dragons want freedom."*

I swallowed. He was wrong. He *had* to be wrong. We were here to restore the Dragon Riders, a thing both elves and dragons benefitted from. *Trust me?*

Zakŏr shook his head and huffed. *"Hear elf thoughts. Friends want me in cage."* He closed his eyes as if in deep thought. *"Khili'thion imagining size of my cage when big. Whips. Blood. Tears."* His eyes opened and bore into my soul. *"Elves keep secrets from Ezerth."*

I stepped away from the cage. Could that be true? My stomach coiled in a knot. Had my whole tribe been lied to about the harmony between elves and dragons, or simply naive enough to believe the bond had come peacefully? I shook my head. There was no time to think about that now. Once I completed this mission, and entered Khili's brotherhood, I could get answers.

I won't let that happen to you. You have to let me help you. If you stay here, you're doomed. If you go with me, you have a chance to see your family again. Don't you like those odds? I prayed the hatchling would see my reasoning, and that he was horribly wrong about my people.

Zakŏr side-eyed the fumbling troll. His blue wings fluttered in the small space and he lowered his head. *"Family gone. Friends only."*

I felt a wave of his grief—too great for such a new creature—

and knelt before the cage. I placed my hand on the bars. *I don't have a family either.* My throat tightened and I numbed myself to the pain of that statement like I had done for years. When our eyes met, all I could see in him was the little boy who'd stumbled into the rogue's guild, crying for food. Who'd attached himself to the guild master, only to be given to Khili at fourteen. Who'd longed to find family in every group he'd been a part of, with no success. This mission *had* to change all of that.

A tear rolled down the hatchling's cheek, and the grief in my chest heightened. He rested his forehead against my hand, the bars separating us. Suddenly, I was in Zakŏr's memories. I saw flashes of a large blue dragon flying overhead, roaring in pain as a goblin spear drove into its throat. A bag was thrown over my vision and I felt the jerks and bumps of a wagon. And then pain, torture, and sorrow.

For the first time in the last several years, tears trickled down my cheeks. I pressed my forehead against the cage, Zakŏr's warmth on the other side.

I'm sorry.

The hatchling purred. *"Zakŏr not hurt elf. Go with Ezerth."*

I cleared my throat to rid myself of the lump, wiped my eyes, and got to work picking the lock to his cage.

The floor rumbled and Zakŏr's eyes widened. *"Goblins in ground come up. Hurry!"*

I fumbled with the clunky lock. No—I needed to calm down. Needed to focus. It would do no good to panic and delay. *Click.* Relief flooded me and I pulled open the cage door. I only had to remove the chain from around his neck.

Zakŏr knocked into me when the ground again shook. I landed on my back with the scaled creature on top of me. His claws dug into my shoulder, and I let out a whimper.

A goblin with dirt crackling off his body emerged from the ground. "Oi! He's got our beasty!"

I swore under my breath and pushed the dragon off of me. There wasn't time to pick the lock on his neck. I gripped the chain and tugged until it lifted off of his head.

"Stop that!" The goblin charged at me as more of his friends emerged from the dirt.

Fly, Zakŏr!

He shoved past me and out of the cage. "*Can't. Too little.*"

Perhaps baby dragons needed to learn to fly like elflings learned to walk. *Fire?*

"*No.*"

So the baby dragon was helpless. Okay—I had to protect him. *Stay behind me.* I brandished my two daggers and shifted my weight, ready to move fast. The first goblin pulled out a jagged sword and lunged at me. I side-stepped and slit his outstretched arm in the same motion. He dropped his sword and cursed at me. *Thunk.* An arrow pierced his back, and he toppled over.

Khili'thion and others in our division flooded through the door. Arrows and balls of fire poured down on our enemies.

I was no longer alone.

Zakŏr nudged my fingers with his snout. "*Elf promised.*"

I know. Stay with me.

"Ezerth, get out of here!" Khili yelled over the onslaught. With the goblins preoccupied fending for their lives against my division, I slipped Zakŏr back out the door and shut it, leaving behind the screams from inside.

The courtyard was still. A soft breeze brushed over the

macabre red graveyard. Goblins and a handful of elves lay dead in the dirt. Though I'd seen battle before, my stomach still churned at the gore. This was just an illustration of the destruction that would happen if Zakŏr fell into the wrong hands. The question was, whose hands were wrong?

If he was right, I couldn't turn him over to my people, but what did a hatchling know? If he was wrong and I let him go free, he could die in the wild, and I could lose all standing.

I guided the dragon through the mire and across the bridge. The silence after death was potent.

We stopped after several rows of trees in the forest. The roar of a waterfall thundered in the distance.

"*Home now.*" The hatchling looked up at me with pure blue eyes, full of innocence and unwarranted trust.

I swallowed. Was that really my call to make? I was just doing my duty. I wasn't meant to ask questions. But then again, what sort of rogue would I truly be if I didn't bend the rules from time to time?

Yes. Home.

We started walking east when the sound of twigs snapping caught my attention. I stepped in front of Zakŏr and reached for my dagger.

Khili'thion jogged into view with a smile piercing through the blood on his face. "Ezerth!"

My hand hovered over the dagger at my side, unsure if goblins followed him.

Khili clasped my back. "You got him!"

The pride I should have felt for bringing the hatchling to my people was lost somewhere in my whirling mind, but I forced out a smile nonetheless. "Where's everyone else?" I peered around him.

"They're still dealing with the goblins. I wanted to make sure you two got out all right." He grinned down at the dragon.

I stood my ground between them. "We aren't going to hurt him, right?"

"Of course not!" Khili ruffled my hair—an act of brotherly affection I'd always longed for. A sense of belonging settled in my chest but was tainted with everything I'd learned that day.

Khili reached down to touch Zakŏr, and the dragon scurried behind my legs, ducking his head.

"*No touch.*"

"I don't think he wants to be manhandled, Khili." I crossed my arms.

Khili frowned. "I wasn't going to *manhandle* him. Simply pet the little guy."

I reached behind me and touched Zakŏr's head. He pushed into my palm like a kitten.

Before I could fully register what was happening, Khili dove for Zakŏr, pulled a spiked metal collar with a leash out from under his cloak, and shoved it on Zakŏr's neck.

"No!" I plowed into Khili and knocked him off of Zakŏr.

Zakŏr shrieked and flapped his wings, which only lifted him a few inches off the ground before he landed again. Coughs of smoke spilled out of his mouth.

Khili and I tumbled in the dirt. I may have been fast, but he was stronger. He pinned me to the ground.

"Let him go!" I screamed up at him.

"Calm down, Ezerth, and I'll let you up. Okay?" He searched my face.

My jaw tightened as anger boiled through me, but I nodded.

True to his word, Khili stood.

I, however, sprang to my feet. Pulling my dagger free, I sliced Khili's arm enough to make him drop the leash, and I caught it before he could retrieve it.

Khili swore at me and pressed down on the wound. "Ezerth!" He swore again, his eyes dark with rage. "We just need to make sure he doesn't run away. Calm down!"

I narrowed my eyes, panting. "If he bonded to us naturally like we've been told, then he wouldn't *want* to escape."

Khili sighed heavily. "Look, boy, we can't take any chances. We need this dragon, and he needs us. He's too stupid and young to understand. Without us, he will grow up to be a monster."

Zakŏr clawed at the ground. He shook out his wings in protest. "*Dragons calm. Fight if beaten.*"

"What proof do you have?" I said to Khili. "Just stories." My knuckles whitened around the leash. Zakŏr had no monstrous feelings about him. I promised I wouldn't let them capture Zakŏr, and what sort of man would I be if I turned my back on the helpless?

"Listen to me. You don't understand how vital this is," Khili continued. "The dragons may have forgotten our bond, but we have not. In time, he will remember it in his veins, and all will be right. He just needs some coaxing for now."

Zakŏr growled behind me. "*Lying. Remember fine. Slaves. Forced bonding. Crying.*"

I looked Khili dead in the eye and said, "If he's forgotten the bond, then how come he's been talking to me in my head ever since I saw him?"

Any pretenses Khili had up before vanished when shock riddled his face. "He's . . . talking to you? That's not possible.

Only Dragon Riders can do that, and you're no such thing. He needs a real Dragon Rider to remain tame."

"*Lies. Dragon talk when want. Or forced.*"

Could it be possible that Khili was deceived too? Were all our people blind to the horrors that had happened in the past? Had we all believed a harmonious lie that disguised the dissonant, violent truth?

I looked down at the leash in my hand. If that were the case, there'd be no use for the leash. No, Khili knew exactly what he was doing, and if this was what it meant to be in his brotherhood, I wanted nothing to do with it.

"You're lying, Khili," I spat.

Khili held his hands up and took a step closer. "Ezerth. Be reasonable. If it weren't for me, you'd still be rotting in the rogue guild. I've given you purpose. You'd be a pathetic monster too if I hadn't saved you. So shut up and do as you're told."

His words were a gut punch, the final blow to any loyalty I felt toward Khili. I pulled a dagger free. "Stay back." I knew Khili, had studied him, and knew his weaknesses. If he tried to take Zakŏr, I would exploit every single one of those weaknesses until the dragon was free. And the uneasy look in his eyes told me he knew it too.

I wasn't proud of what I had planned, but it was the only way to keep the dragon safe, and Khili would be just fine. *Waterfall to the east. Run.*

Zakŏr nudged my palm. "*Friend. Come?*"

There was no home for me among the elves anymore. *Yes. Run.* I dropped the leash and Zakŏr took off behind me.

A good rogue always carries a slew of knives and daggers,

and I was no exception. I flicked throwing knives into both of Khili's feet and drove my dagger into his right thigh. He gasped and clutched his bloodied leg.

"Zakŏr doesn't need a Dragon Rider. He has me," I hissed into Khili's face and pushed him onto his back. I was certain he would try to follow, but with the location of the injuries I'd inflicted, he wouldn't get far.

I turned and sprinted after Zakŏr. An arrow with blue fletching whizzed past my head and my stomach dropped. That was meant to be a kill shot, and if Khili hadn't been injured lying on the ground, I knew it would have been. Khili would end me over this if he had the chance. He was no better than the goblins.

Zakŏr and I ran—I had to slow my pace to match his stubby legs—until we reached the ledge where the waterfall poured into a large pool. Khili's shouts echoed behind us and more arrows flew. Zakŏr and I jumped from the ledge and plunged into the water below.

My tribe hunted a slave I'd given everything to rescue: a dragon hatchling named Zakŏr. As we swam for the water's edge, I decided I'd give my life to return him to his home.

ACKNOWLEDGMENTS

Thank you to the team of editors, beta readers, authors, and so many more people who poured their time and energy into this book. Thanks be to the God who answers prayers in His timing and in His will.

—Anne J. Hill and Moriah Chavis

ABOUT THE AUTHORS

ANNE J. HILL is an author who enjoys writing fantasy for all ages. Her love of words has led to her career as an editor and content writer. She runs Twenty Hills Publishing with the help of her circus performing best friend: Lara E. Madden, and horror enthusiast: AudraKate Gonzalez. She spends her days dreaming up fantastical realms, researching ways to get away with murder...for her books, arguing over commas at the kitchen table, talking out loud to the characters in her head, promising her housemate that she isn't, in fact, crazy, and rearranging her personal library—affectionately dubbed the "Book Dungeon."

Instagram @anne.j.hill.editing
www.annejhill.com

MORIAH CHAVIS is the author of the young adult fantasy *Heart of the Sea* and various short stories. Her next novel, A YA speculative mystery, is coming from Twenty Hills Publishers September 2025. She is a two-time graduate from the University of South Carolina with a Bachelor's in Liberal Arts and a Master's in Library and Information Science. It's been said you can find perusing bookstores, attempting to persuade strangers to read her favorite books, oscillating between watching *The Lord of the Rings* trilogy (her husband's favorite) or *Harry Potter* (hers), and keeping her books from the clutches of her two feisty cats.

Ashley Schaller is an award winning author who prefers tea over coffee, will never say no to puppy snuggles, and proudly wears the title of "Dog Mom". When not writing, she can often be found reading her next favorite book, baking, obsessing over owls (but only the cute cartoon ones), or learning new crochet patterns.

As a writer, she seeks to create stories that glorify God. Stories that entertain, but you never have to worry about the content. To connect with Ashley and stay updated on all things books and writing, follow her on Instagram @ashleyschallerauthor

 AUDRAKATE GONZALEZ started writing horror stories when she ran out of Goosebumps books to read as a child. While she will always love horror, she decided to branch out and write something lighter for this anthology. She has a BA in Creative Writing and is working on her MFA. AudraKate's other published works are her first novel, *Tomato Juice*, and a short story called "Imagination." She lives in Ohio with her handsome husband, and her adorable furry bad boys, Zero and Scrappy Doo. When AudraKate isn't writing, you can find her reading, watching scary movies or sleeping.

HANNAH CARTER is just a girl who still wakes up every day hoping to figure out she's secretly a mermaid. Along with *Saltwater Souls*, Hannah has also written *The Atlantis Trilogy* (published through SnowRidge Press), which contains even more mermaids, magic, and murder. Her short stories and award-winning flash fiction pieces have been published in various anthologies, including all of Twenty Hills's. She has also won Editor's Choice Award from Havok Publishing twice, for her pieces in the *Prismatic* and *World Tour* anthologies. In 2022, her flash fiction piece, "A Home for Nova," won a Realm Award. Hannah also won a competition with her short story, "Lara." In addition to fiction, she also has had over a dozen devotionals published in various magazines, as well as six devotions published in *Finding God in Anime.* In her spare time, she's probably either cuddling her cats, drinking tea, reading, or practicing for her imaginary Broadway debut. Connect with her on Instagram at @mermaidhannahwrites.

BROOKE J. KATZ is a stay at home/homeschooling mom by day and author/poet by night. Jesus and Lyons tea fuel her. Writing and painting have been a way for her to step into another world and for her work to be an outlet for someone else to find encouragement, or just some time to themselves being lost in a story. She is known to always have a book on her and dropping what she's doing to pray. You can find her on IG/Goodreads @Brookejkatz or her website https://brookejkatz.wixsite.com/brookejkatz

Morgan J. Manns is a speculative fiction writer who enjoys crafting enchanting worlds and captivating magic systems, a skill she nurtures after tucking her children into bed. Her imagination is fueled by the works of Brandon Sanderson, Patrick Rothfuss, and Samantha Shannon, serving as constant inspiration. By day, Morgan works as an English teacher, seeking ways to ignite the writing potential in her students while helping them uncover the transformative power of the written word. When she's not writing, or teaching about writing, she can be found chasing after her two young children, delving into fantasy novels alongside her husband, or exploring the breathtaking Canadian vistas surrounding her home. One of her favorite pastimes is canoeing with her family on the glistening lake just behind her house.

A lover of all things magical, MARY E. DIPPLE uses her talent of spinning stories, to shine a light into the darkness that so easily entangles our lives. When Mary isn't slaying the darkness with story, she enjoys spending her days tending her ever growing rose garden, playing with her lovable furry assistants, and writing flash fiction. You can find many of her flash fiction pieces on her website at www.marydipple.com.

 H. L. DAVIS is a Christian, wife, and homeschool mom who calls the South home. She has written and published multiple short stories both in print and online, primarily with Havok Publishing and Twenty Hills. When she isn't brainstorming ideas and weaving words into stories, she enjoys reading, graphic design, and quality time with her family and friends. You can find her on Instagram @h.l.davis_stories or on her Substack, hldavisstories.substack.com.

Holly Maley writes stories inspired by saints, fairy tales, and myths. She has a degree in Writing from the University of Victoria but learned more about storytelling by listening to strange podcasts about stranger tales. Her stories dance on the intersection of the old and the new, capturing the wisdom and depth of ancient tales and the whimsy and drama of modern ones. You can find her awkwardly navigating the internet at @hollylynnmaley.

B.R.R. CANNON has always loved writing and storytelling. While fantasy and sci-fi are her staples, she also dabbles in other genres including poetry and nonfiction. She has previously published stories with Spark Flash Fiction, Havok, Nightshade Publishing, and Twenty Hills Publishing. Currently, she's working on her debut time travel novel. When she's not creating imaginary worlds, she enjoys drinking Darjeeling, finding excuses to wear costumes, and spending time with her husband, children, and cat.

KAYLA E. GREEN is an author and poet who writes to remind others—and herself—that light always prevails over darkness. When she isn't writing, reading, or spending time with her family, she loves singing loudly and off-key to KLove Radio and pretending she's a unicorn. She has written an award-winning YA fantasy novella, *Aivan: The One Truth*, and an inspirational poetry collection, *Metamorphosis*. Kayla also has stories and poems featured in various anthologies as well as contest-winning stories published in Clean Fiction Magazine and with WOW! Women On Writing. Additionally, she has several flash fiction stories available through Havok Publishing. Kayla's next YA fantasy novel is set to debut in 2025. Learn more and connect with her at theunicornwriter.com and on Instagram @theunicornwriter93.

SAMANTHA MENDELL is a firm believer in Truth and fairy tales. As a storyteller, she weaves fantastical tales of unexpected heroes who find hope in the most unlikely places. She's published several short stories and is currently finishing her debut novel. She resides in Nashville, Tennessee with her Jedi husband and works as a full-time freelance editor.

Rienne French writes fantasy, sci-fi, and horror. Being dyslexic, her stories all start in her sketchbook. Whether she is inking an illustration or writing a flash fiction, it is the art of storytelling that Rienne loves. Her favorite stories always feature a mysterious monster. When she isn't not writing or drawing, you can find Rienne playing games with her children or watching old monster movies with her husband.

Megan E. Parmerter grew up as a Navy kid, living and traveling in multiple states and countries. One constant throughout those travels was a book in her hand. She wrote and illustrated her own stories at a young age, and she tackled her first novels in middle and high school. It wasn't until she came to Christ, however, that she found that writing might not be simply a hobby, but a calling. In response to that calling, she wrote 53, a personal story influenced by her own struggles as well as the death of her brother from leukemia. Now she's working to create a world where more of her stories can not only entertain but speak truth into the lives of young readers. She lives in Pennsylvania with her husband and two children, juggling her writing with homesteading and entirely too many crafty hobbies.

AUSTIN D. ANDERSON is a storyteller, a high school English teacher, and an adventurer who has traveled as far as the Mountain Kingdom of Lesotho (Africa). He and his wife are the proud parents of a two-year-old and another on the way! The "D" in his pen name is short for "David," his father's name. After David's unexpected passing (due to cancer) in early 2024, Austin dedicated all of his future literary works to him. Like his father, Austin's stories illuminate hope even in the darkest of circumstances.

AMANDA AULER writes young adult fantasy stories that explore emotional growth and personal resilience. When she's not at her laptop, she can be found baking, improving her ASL fluency, and trying to keep up with her four growing boys. She and her husband live in central North Carolina where they stay up too late watching anime and eating cookies.